WAS SHE REAL?

Charles looked down at the unconscious girl. The girl who'd worked with him, loved him. He turned to the other man.

"What have you done to Sara, Hiram? What's this all about?"

From his pocket, Hiram Dinkuhl took a small knife; he flipped the catch and the sapphire blade leaped out. Charles watched in fascination as the other man bent down toward the unconscious face. Charles heard himself saying: "Stop. . . !"

With a deft motion, Dinkuhl sliced into the flesh at the base of the girl's forehead. He held up the strip he had cut away. There was no bleeding from the incision. The cut laid bare not flesh but plastic.

Now, beyond any doubt, Charles knew he had been loving a mask . . . .

John Christopher

PLANET IN PERIL

An Avon Original

AVON BOOK DIVISION
The Hearst Corporation
959 Eighth Avenue—New York 19, N.Y.

Planet in Peril

PART ONE

I

AFTER HE HAD PUT the remains of the meal down the chute and snapped the table back into the wall, Charles Grayner slumped automatically in his fireside chair and his eyes, as automatically, went to the flickering telescreen. He cut the whole thing off when he left the house in the morning, but the daily help put it on again. He knew her viewing habits by now; she alternated between three channels—Red League, Honey, and Cosy Bright. The singer, Loulou del Keith, was a Cosy Bright exclusive. His hand dropped to the control panel. He checked himself for a moment and then pressed the ninth button decisively.

Sight and sound went, and were replaced by a Mozart string quartet. On the screen was the El Greco "Cleansing of the Temple." Dinkuhl had used that juxtaposition before—twice at least. Charles felt a mild irritation; he had been one of those who had protested against this business of deliberately associating musical works and paintings.

The quartet ended, on a flat note. Dinkuhl's face came through, characteristically smiling, half mocking, half enraged.

"This," Dinkuhl said, "is Channel KF." His voice was soft but flexible; it could resonate into anger. "I propose to save a lot of people a lot of money. Well, when I say a *lot* of people—" He shrugged. "I've hired a boy to go

9

through my stenoflips for me. He has instructions to destroy any one that tells me I have to stop linking Mozart and El Greco, or Haydn and Rubens, or Beethoven and Rembrandt. So save yourself a couple of quarters."

He paused. "Do you object that you would prefer to see the musicians, in all their ugliness, in all their squalor? In that case I recommend that you go right out and see them—in the flesh, my friends, in the disillusioning flesh. Few of you will have to travel more than five hundred miles to find a concert hall. But this is TV, and there is only one Channel KF, and I shall continue to kill two birds with one stone. Some of you, at least, must be tone deaf."

Dinkuhl backed away from the camera, turned his back on it, and rooted around in a corner of the studio. Then he came back to face the camera. "Now I remember," he said. "I fixed it all up before. Ladies and gentlemen, the KF newsreel!"

The music was a neat parody of the signature tune for the Red League newsreel, in a minor key, mocking. The screen showed the night sky, caught the Moon, and dissolved into a familiar moonscape—the view from the Tycho observatory.

"Out there," Dinkuhl said, "along with mystery, there is beauty. Let us look not at a new planet but at the —the—new comet."

The screen was patterned with brilliant stars; the bright smudge of the comet was central, beneath Jupiter.

"More than two thousand years ago this great comet last swept in its parabola round the sun. While eighty generations of men have come and gone, while the human race has climbed so painfully to its present eminence, that majestic luminary has been plodding round a course trillions of miles away in the outer dark."

The camera came back to Dinkuhl's own face. He lowered his head so that light gleamed from the bald patch at the crown, and smiled up from under bushy eyebrows.

10

"I suggest you get up out of that goddam chair, and go outside and have a look for yourself. Channel KF proposes to help you on your way by closing down for half an hour. We are going out on the roof to have a look at the comet ourself. Good-bye."

The screen went blank. Charles got up, found his field-glasses and went out into the night air, damp and a little frosty.

He made his way down the path to the point, beyond the arbor, where his view of the sky would be uninterrupted. He raised his glasses and found the comet. He looked at it until his arm began to ache and his hand shook the glasses. Nothing much—a smear of whiteness, with one of the planet's moons set in it like a pearl.

He was preparing to go back to the house when he heard the loud ring of the call amplifier; automatically he quickened his step and then, deliberately, slowed again. He pressed the door open, and cut the amplifier out. The din dropped to the usual persistent buzz.

In the lounge, he pressed the button for the information panel on the callscreen. The letters sprang into being at the left-hand side, ran across, and jerked back again, in a never-ending series:

GRAYNER FROM LEDBETTER—UC DIV HQ DETROIT—UR-
CENT URGENT PERSONAL GRAYNER FROM LEDBETTER—

Ledbetter. He wasted no time in putting the callscreen on reply circuit. While his Accept call was going out he pulled a chair over and sat down. He tried to be at ease, reminding himself that at thirty-eight he was past the stage of being upset by unexpected calls from HQ. At least, he should be.

It was not Ledbetter, of course, who took the call. A young man, with a sleek look and the little rubylite badges on his lapels, spelling out United Chemicals, smiled.

"Grayner?" he said. "We haven't met, have we? I'm Official Paulton."

"Glad to know you," Charles said evenly.

"Manager Ledbetter wants to see you; he asked me to fix an appointment. Can you get here in the morning?"

"All right."

"Ten hundred. Look me up first. My room is F 73. You know your way around the place, I take it?"

"I've been there before."

"See you then."

Paulton let his smile fade into a look of sober concentration, and then switched off. The callscreen blanked. Charles sat where he was for several minutes. The first thing he told himself was that there was no point at all in trying to work out possible reasons for the call to see Ledbetter. From that stage, nevertheless, he went on to do precisely that.

His niche in the Saginaw laboratories was a small but apparently secure one. If this were a demotion—a removal back, perhaps, to the general lab—it was difficult to see why he should be called urgently in to Detroit to be informed of it. That was a routine matter and would be dealt with through routine channels. It would not need an interview with Ledbetter to confirm it.

The same argument applied to the suggestion that there might be a promotion for him. There could be no justification. Sixteen years' research in the radioactive properties of diamonds had not, he knew, fitted him for the control of any larger project. One assistant and two lab boys. After sixteen years you could do that, and that was all you could do.

That left him up in the air. No demotion, no promotion—then why the call to Detroit?

At precisely ten hundred the following morning Paulton looked puzzled when he saw Charles' face. Charles was standing in the corridor outside room 73 on F floor and the small inset callscreen transmitted his features to the panel on the wall facing Paulton's desk. Then Paulton's face cleared.

12

"Grayner, of course! Come on in."

The door beside him slid open, and closed after him as he went through. Paulton had genuine interest and recollection on his face when they met in the flesh. His control, Charles reflected, was admirable; many would have overdone the forgetfulness. He shook hands with a warm grip. Ledbetter's rooms, of course, were on B. Paulton led him through to the room marked *Manager G. D. Ledbetter*, and whistled at the door. It opened, and they went in. Ledbetter was talking into a dictaphone. He looked up grimly as they entered, but went on to finish the stenoflip he was engaged on. Then he said to Paulton:

"I propose to have the sound-key changed on that door. When I do I shall make a point of not letting you in on the new one. Who's this?"

"Grayner," Paulton said. "It won't make a lot of difference—about the door. Grayner. You told me to get him here to see you."

Ledbetter said: "Yes, of course. All right, you can go, Harry. Next time you come in, use the callscreen."

Paulton, retreating, said: "I'll try to remember."

Charles had been studying Ledbetter. He had seen him on newsreels and in the UC telezine, but those had been formal occasions. Now he was entirely friendly and relaxed. He had got his managership young and his present seniority had been reached in a vault over several more likely shoulders. He said to Charles: "You'll be wondering why I've got you to come along here."

Charles said: "Well, naturally. And the notice was rather short."

Ledbetter nodded. "The reason I wanted to see you is that I am in the middle of the usual thing that new Area Managers go in for. I'm having a reorganization." He looked directly at Charles. "You will have noticed some of the earlier changes in your own plant?"

Charles nodded. "I'd hoped maybe I was in too small a niche to be noticed."

From one of the drawers in his desk Ledbetter pro-

13

duced a microfilm capsule and clipped it into the projector. The telescreen on the wall lit up and displayed what was immediately recognizable as one of Charles' own recent reports—*The effect of zeta irradiation on the photoelectric properties of a type II diamond (Cape white)*.

"You write a very fair report. But you're not ambitious?"

"You have my psychoplan."

Ledbetter smiled. "Frankly, an error was made in your case. You aren't really the dead-end type."

"You didn't call me in simply to offer condolences—official or otherwise?"

Ledbetter said: "Now, let's get it straight and lay it on the table. Alpha—I'm in a mood for change. Beta—you should never have been tossed into that lab in the first place. Gamma's the rub. Gamma—you've spent sixteen years messing around with radio-active diamonds. That restricts the possibilities of what we can do with you to a somewhat startling extent."

Charles said: "Very interesting. Delta?"

"Coincidence," said Ledbetter, "rears its ungainly but attractive head. There's a little place going at a spot called San Miguel. South of San Diego. Area HQ is at Los Angeles—a guy called Mettrill. You'll like him. And you will be picking up some interesting threads. This for intance."

He removed the microfilm of Charles' report and replaced it with another. The report unfolded itself before them. In the list of references at the end there were half a dozen papers of his own. He looked at Ledbetter.

"Where was this published?"

"It hasn't been."

"Because?"

"Because that is one of the advantages of your new post. Don't publish if you don't want to. You might call yourself a scientific hobo, with endowment."

Charles' mind had been engaged with the paper that

14

had just been projected for him. Things began to click into place.

"Do I come under Contact Section?" he asked.

Ledbetter smiled. "No."

Charles said patiently: "Then it will be all right for me to publish whatever I want?"

"I didn't say that. The new job is restricted. You are under San Diego for admin but any reports you make go direct to Graz."

"To Tapron?"

"To Nikku-Tsi, for Preston."

"And what do they want me to turn out?"

"I'm not in the secret. This report of Humayun's you've just seen—it doesn't mean anything to me because it's not my line, but I suspect that there isn't anything vital in it anyway, or I wouldn't have been given it to show you."

Charles said: "It's fairly routine stuff, as a matter of fact. Bombardment conductivity; we've done a certain amount at Saginaw." Ledbetter nodded his appreciation. "There are one or two points in it, though—"

"They, I take it, were meant to whet your appetite. Do they?"

"Yes." He hesitated before he shot the next question at the Manager. "What became of my predecessor? Radiation poisoning or the managerial variety?"

"A good question. Humayun, I understand, was by way of being an amateur sailor like myself—plenty of scope in a place like that as I've indicated. I don't know the details of what happened, except that his boat came back, keel upwards, and he didn't. It's a tricky coast, I understand." Charles thought for a moment that he looked at him oddly, but there wasn't enough in it to get hold of a meaning. "A very tricky coast. I should stay away from it when the flow tide's getting near the turn."

Charles nodded. "When do you want me to start?"

Ledbetter glanced at the note-pad inset on the desk under his right hand. "You will be turning your gyro in at Saginaw. We'll pick you up with your things in the

15

morning and you'll join the ten hundred stratoliner here. By the way, in your new position you are up five hundred a month. You qualify for a Cat C gyro *and* limousine, too. One other triviality—you don't object to ex-Siraqis?"

Charles looked at him with some surprise. "How many of them?"

"Only one. Humayun was, and he picked one for his assistant. I have the impression that a lot of the valuable side of Humayun's work may only be traceable through her."

"I don't see any reason why I should want to get rid of her."

"That's fine, then." Ledbetter glanced at the chronometer on the wall. "You'll have some packing to do, so I won't keep you any longer."

Charles left the UC HQ building in the first place because he wanted to drop in, for the last time, on Stone's, the little gramophone record exchange at the corner of 27th and Main. He browsed through the shelves of assorted records near the door. He found a set of the Munich John Passion, with one record missing, and wondered whether it was worth while taking it in the hope of filling in the gap some time in the future. But it was priced too low; that represented Stone's own considered opinion that the odds against were very high. He put the records back as someone came into the shop.

He recognized Dinkuhl, of course. The odd thing was that Dinkuhl recognized him; they had been introduced once, some years before, in circumstances that were now vague.

The proprietor of Channel KF said: "Charlie Grayner! Nice to find you again. Having a last look round before you light out for the land of sunshine?"

They shook hands. Charles said:

"You astonish me."

Dinkuhl grinned. "You don't show it."

"You do, though. I suppose it would be rude to ask you where you got your information from?"

16

"It must be six or seven years since I saw you." Dinkuhl shook his head, clearly delighted with his own powers of recollection. "At the Sullivan place, before they got a transfer to Melbourne. It is you who are going to California, isn't it? I thought it must be. Source of information? That, Charlie, is one thing you never ask a TV man. Come back with me and have a glass of something."

Charles nodded. "Thanks."

Dinkuhl's house, about a mile away, overlooking Lake Erie, was twentieth-century Scandinavian in architecture, but had apparently been more soundly constructed than the average. Dinkuhl led Charles upstairs to a large room on the first floor, with a view on to the lake, and brought him a drink in a very fine-looking wide-bowled glass.

Dinkuhl held his own glass up. "Cheers," he said.

They drank. The taste was odd. Charles held the glass up in inquiry.

"What is it, Manager?"

"Call me Hiram," Dinkuhl said. "You like it? It's a little something I knocked up myself. Turnip-and-tomato wine. Not bad, though? Not at all bad."

Answering his own question, he simultaneously topped up both their glasses. He fished out of one pocket the old-fashioned spectacles he sometimes wore in the studio and put them on to study Charles more closely.

"Well, then," he said. "What are you going to do for culture in the Far West? You're one of the customers—you wrote me a letter about a month back."

"I can give up TV," Charles said. He smiled. "Even KF. I might take up reading."

"It is an unhappy fact," Dinkuhl said, "that the only people who can give up TV are precisely those who commonly patronize KF. Well, I guess it may last out my time."

"I never did understand why Telecom let you keep running."

"For only one reason, but a good one. Our charter got

17

incorporated, in some strange way, in their constitution. I give the credit to my then predecessor, a guy called Bert White. The proprietorship of KF is a self-perpetuating office for which the chief qualification is low cunning, but White was exceptional. Short of rewriting their own constitution, a desperate step that might stir up a regular horde of hibernating skeletons, they've got to go on giving us rights of telecasting. They just have to get what satisfaction they can from watching us slowly fade away; but since we represent one of the few remaining strands of capitalism in the modern world, there's one line I can try. Under managerialism, we're sunk. So I shall try switching us to the one tiny oasis where managerialism doesn't send its camels—to Siraq."

"Well, good luck." Charles thought about it for a moment. "Not very hopeful, is it?"

Dinkuhl said: "I like you, Charlie. You put things well. I can always join Red League again—you know I started with that outfit?"

"No. I didn't know."

"The day I tossed my Telecom membership card in the lake was the happiest day of my life. I'm not even sure which lake it was now. I suppose they would make me out a new one."

Dinkuhl glanced at his watch; it was extraordinarily big and he wore it on his wrist instead of on his watch-finger.

"But pending Siraq or Red League, the show must go on. So, on your way. One thing." Charles looked at him. "I hear the boating's tricky on that coast."

Charles said: "I've already been told that."

"This," said Dinkuhl, "is official. The voice of the KF News Reel."

II

SARA KOUPAL DID NOT make a good initial impression on
Charles. She was attractive enough, dark, rather square-
faced, but her personality was unattractive. It was com-
forting to remember that Ledbetter had told him he
need not keep her if he didn't want to.

The lab was on high ground, facing the sea and perhaps a hundred yards from it. There was a good view of
San Miguel, which was about a mile away, and the back
looked into an orange grove which appeared to stretch
indefinitely. The equipment in the lab was very good.
The first thing he noticed was the five-thousand KV
electrobombard he had asked for, and failed to get,
when it was announced a year before. There were three
cyclotrons. Money had been spent here, and he felt he
knew UC policy well enough to be sure that that meant
they had expected to get something out of it. The difficulty was finding precisely what.

Humayun's notes were scrappy; scrappy enough to be
just about useless and yet, tantalizingly, not quite
scrappy enough to discard entirely. It was the kind of
work, clearly enough, which would gain considerably in
meaning with the application of the key of what
Humayun was driving at.

This need obliged him to fall back on Sara. He found
her in the north room, engaged in the graphitization of a
specimen of carbon. He stood behind her without saying
anything for a couple of minutes. He said at last:

"And the next step?"

She turned round slowly, holding a pair of asbestos

19

tongs. She looked at him steadily, and behind the steadiness she was obviously jumpy and hostile.

"Slow bombardment, drying out for twenty-four hours, and checking lattice changes by positron diffraction."

"To establish?"

She hesitated; she still looked at him but her gaze was edgy. "It's a continuation of a series of experiments Dr. Humayun put in hand."

It was a warm day outside. Charles said impulsively: "I'd like to have a talk with you, Sara. You can spare half an hour?"

She said distantly: "If you'd prefer that."

They walked down to the shore in silence. To the south there was something of an anchorage—a rough breakwater with a couple of concrete posts built on.

He nodded toward them. "What became of the boat?"

She was still standing, as though awaiting orders. He said: "We might as well sit down, I guess," and she sat on a stone a few feet from the one he took.

She smoothed her skirt down and looked not at him but away out to sea. "The boat? They took it away."

"They?"

"Your friends." She glanced at him. "Contact Section."

He said, slowly:

"We might as well get some things clear at the start. I'm not Contact Section, and I haven't been briefed by Contact Section. I've been doing a very ordinary job in diamond research under Detroit Sector, and I've been pulled in here apparently because they wanted someone in a hurry. I'd hoped you might be able to help me . . . I'm pretty much in the dark all the way round."

"It was most inconsiderate of Dai," she said, "to get drowned without first leaving you detailed instructions."

"I'm sorry." He looked at her averted face, trying to gauge the kind of emotion responsible for the bitterness of her remarks. "I'm probably not putting things very well. You see, I didn't know Dr. Humayun. One can't—"

He thought for a moment she might be going to smile. She said, more gently than she had spoken so far:

20

"You still aren't putting them very well, are you? You're right that you can't be expected to feel very sorry for someone you never knew, but at least when you are talking about him you can give him his title—as you finally did."

He looked at her in astonishment; then he understood.

"There's no disrespect," Charles said, "in not giving a man his title here. Scientific titles are very rarely used, anyway. There was really no offense meant." He smiled ruefully. "In fact, I wasn't even being accidentally rude, though I believe I often am."

She said: "I'm sorry." She studied his face. She had a direct and honest look and for the moment her nervousness had gone. "What is it you want to know?"

He looked at her helplessly. "Primarily, what I am supposed to do. You seem to have a line to follow. It's somewhat embarrassing that I haven't."

The mistrust was there again, and stronger. "It's hard to swallow—that they should appoint you in Dai's place and not tell you what you were expected to do."

"All the same," Charles said. "I'd like you to make the effort." He paused. "It may make a difference that I've been rushed straight here from Detroit. I gather you are implying that Graz knew what's up, but that doesn't mean Detroit does. I suppose Graz may finally wake up to the need for telling me. I suppose I could telecall Nikko-Tsi and jog their memories, but in my experience it's always better to get along on your own if you can. Pestering HQ can have unfortunate results."

She wrinkled her brow. "Am I being dumb again? Is that a usual sort of thing to happen in a managerial?"

"Not unusual. Why do you think all the original work is now being done in Taifa and El-Majalem?"

She was pleased and surprised. "You see that, too?"

"They that have eyes can see. Now—this job?"

She hesitated for a second, then said firmly: "Dai Humayun was after a new power source, on a photoelectric basis. He had reached the stage where he could see things a lot more clearly, but there was still a good deal of work to be done."

"Power . . ." Charles said. "Photoelectric . . . ? For the first time I have an inkling. Selenium obviously—germanium and diamond?"

"Long-term irradiation of type III diamonds induces a fundamental structural change—the refractive index—"

"I saw that report. I thought it was a blind for something else. Type III diamond—that's new on me."

"Type III signifies those stones which *do* respond in that way to prolonged irradiation. There aren't many, but they seem to come indiscriminately from type I and type II groups. The germanium, incidentally, is in because of the structural similarity to diamond. As far as I know it never gave anything. But Dai didn't find it easy to explain the lines he was following. He was still working on germanium."

"And titania?"

"We tried a few things with titania. No soap. The greater refractive index in the raw state doesn't help at all. It's a structural matter."

"So it's a power source," Charles said. "That explains a few things at least. It explains why it was such a rush job getting me down here and also—" He looked at Sara with attention. "Did you know the information had got out—outside UC, I mean?"

She said bitterly: "Does it explain an overturned boat drifting back to shore?"

Gloomily Charles surveyed his cigarette. "Whatever it is, I'm in it, up to the neck." The impact of her last words came properly home to him. "Look, are you suggesting Humayun was murdered?"

She was silent for a moment. "I talk too much," she said at last. "I suppose it doesn't matter now. I've already had my say to Contact Section. It makes no difference—you might as well know what I think. Dai learned his sailing in the Mediterranean. The day he was drowned . . . there was a fair swell but nothing that would be likely to worry him unduly."

22

"Accidents do happen. And Ledbetter told me it was a tricky coast."

She said: "Dai never thought it particularly tricky: he had been sailing it for some years."

"If you think that, why the objection to Contact Section? Surely you're not suggesting they had anything to do with it? UC would hardly be likely to kill the goose just when it's getting broody. Why didn't you tell them what you thought about Humayun's death?"

"I did."

He was surprised. "And?"

"They would not take it seriously. They reported accidental death."

"That doesn't make them your enemies. They might just be mistaken—if your view's the right one."

Her eyes were cold and unfriendly again. "I was under the impression that the job of Contact Sections was to go into anything that might be to the disadvantage of their managerial."

He said easily: "These are slack times, even for Contact Sections. It's rare to find a job done properly nowadays."

He felt a twofold relief. That there was so simple an explanation of her antipathy to Contact Section, and that the predecessor had, after all, simply got himself drowned. The phantasmagoric mists were clearing, leaving behind a familiar and recognizable world framing an ordinary hysterical girl, instead of a nightmare situation pivoting on murder.

She said: "And got out—where?"

"Got out?"

Her voice was impatient. "You said just now—that the information had got out. I suppose, about our work here?"

"That? Yes. It seems to have done. At least, I had the impression that something was known—I don't know how much."

"Inside UC—or another managerial?"

"Strictly speaking, another managerial. Telecom."

23

"And this was in Detroit. Didn't it seem odd to you that Ledbetter should be in the dark, and whoever it was, not?"

"Not really. I didn't mean to imply that he necessarily knew anything more than Ledbetter did. And Ledbetter wasn't entirely in the dark, of course; he knew it was restricted work and had one of Humayun's reports on his desk—not that it conveyed anything to him."

The interview, he realized, had changed its course. His intention had been to question Sara; now, with the bit well between her teeth, Sara was questioning him. The problem was to ease her off the subject without upsetting her further.

He thought he could see how the conversation might be turned; if he could divert the subject to Sara herself.

He said: "Why do people—you, for instance, and Humayun—come over from Siraq in the first place? Faith in the managerial idea? Or what? Not just for the flesh-pots, I take it?"

"People come over for both those reasons. There are always some students who find the system in operation across the border more attractive than that at home. And the standard of personal comfort is less high in Siraq. There's a third reason as well, though. My father came over as a political refugee, and I came with him."

"Political refugee?" It was hard to get hold of a term that had ceased to be valid, in the major world, a century before. He saw Sara smile, understanding his bewilderment. "In what way?"

"It would be difficult to explain. Men conspire as much in Siraq as they do here, but in rather different ways. Daddy was in some plot to overthrow the government, and the plot was discovered. He would have been imprisoned if he had stayed."

Charles said apologetically: "I'm afraid I don't even know what kind of government you have in Siraq. It's not a monarchy, is it?"

"In the true sense of the word, yes. A one-man rule.

The President has the advice of the Sinarqim, but he doesn't need to take the advice."

Charles thought of asking what the Sinarqim might be, and then thought better of it. Something else struck him.

"Your father was mixed up in a plot against the President? And Humayun?"

"Yes. Dai was in it, too."

"Then, if there was something fishy about his death, might it not be that—"

She interrupted decisively. "No. It would only have been imprisonment if they had stayed. We are not a primitive people. And, anyway, it was Daddy who was one of the leaders of the plot; Dai played only a very minor part in it." Her eyes were on a hydroplane, skimming across the ocean's middle distance.

"It's only here that the innocent are killed, simply because they get in somebody's way."

Charles saw no advantage in arguing with an obsession. She had been thawing, perceptibly thawing, and his only concern was to have the process continue.

"Your father?" he asked. "Does he like it over here?"

She shrugged. "Better than prison. He teaches History at Berkeley."

"History?"

"Yes." She smiled. "There still are some who take it. He has two students at present. He gets paid a little less than"—she gestured towards the laboratory—"than Luke does. But he has modest needs. He seems to enjoy life fairly well."

Charles got up. "We could be getting back to see how Luke and Tony are progressing."

They were walking up the pebbled path when she said:

"I suppose they gave you a free hand about me?"

"A free hand?"

"You don't have to keep me here if you don't want to?"

He hesitated. "No. But I can think of no reason why I should want to get rid of you."

She smiled. "Especially since Dai didn't make the right kind of notes. Well?"

They both laughed. A moment later her foot slipped on the loose stones, and he had to catch her to prevent her falling. It was precisely the right contact, at the right time.

One of the skills that Charles had bothered to acquire was that of grinding his own diamonds, instead of depending on having the work done outside. He had gone into the matter with a thoroughness that was natural to him, and had found that certain cuts, which for undiscoverable reasons had been allowed to disappear from use, gave a far greater effect of brilliance than the ones currently fashionable. He explained this to Sara when she showed him one of the stones which had formed the basis of Humayun's report on the refractive index changes in type III diamonds. She held the stone in a narrow pencil of light and they both had to turn their eyes from molten brilliance reflected from it. Charles took the stone and examined it.

"Rose cut. A brilliant cut would give you double the fire. And there was a mid-Twentieth-century improvement, the Brown-brilliant, that does even better."

She looked at him with surprise. He went on. "The stones are cut before irradiation, of course? Did you ever try irradiating them first and then cutting?"

"Yes. It goes dead. Whatever form the lattice change takes, it can't be very stable."

Charles nodded. "Not surprising. And the battery—a simple heat—electricity conversion? What about shielding?"

"Sapphire."

"Yes. Just what was it needed ironing out, Sara?"

"A lot of things. The shielding's a long way from being perfect, and the mirror system is still primitive. In fact, there's only the idea so far. All the development has to be done."

Charles turned over the small diamond in his hand,

examining it. "The development . . . yes, I get that." He looked at Sara. "Imagine for a moment that you are running United Chemicals. You get something like this underway. You—lose your research man, but the thing has reached this stage, anyway. What do you do next?"

"Turn it over to the engineers. It's obvious, isn't it?"

Charles nodded. "You certainly don't get another research man in to do what has been done already. So the question remains—why me? Can you think of a reason why they haven't turned this over to Design Section?"

"No. I wondered about it while Dai was alive. I asked him what he thought about it."

"And he said—"

"He had a poor opinion of the people at Graz. As far as I could gather, he thought they just didn't understand what we were doing. It seems difficult to believe."

"Quite possible, though, I'm afraid. Dai"—he saw her glance at him with pleasure—"would know more about their reactions than you or I. I suppose you didn't see his confidential reports?"

She pointed toward the microfilm files. "Only those on work done. Not the actual memoranda to Nikko-Tsi."

"And the memoranda? Are they on file?"

"They were. Contact Section took them."

He shook his head. "Not that it matters a great deal. I don't think there's anything I can do but piece the picture together, and then send it in with a recommendation that they push it through to Detroit or Milan."

Sara said slowly: "I hope you won't make up your mind too quickly."

"I shall have to get the hang of things properly before I can recommend anything," Charles said.

She said: "You could try the irradiation out on a brilliant-cut stone. I'd like you to have a look at the plan for the selenium rectifier. I've had some ideas which I've incorporated into the scheme as Dai left it."

Without waiting for his reply, she flicked the lights off and dropped a microfilm in the reader. The telescreen on the wall lit up. She demonstrated with a pointer on the small inset screen in the bench, drawing circles round the salient points, circles which, reproduced on the big screen, glowed for perhaps a minute before fading out.

"This is the original scheme. I thought if we made this linkage"—two ellipses joined and became a circle—"and cut out the third stage here . . ."

She pressed a button and a new print appeared on the screen.

"It would look like this. That should boost it."

Charles said: "Yes. That's a pretty piece of work. Very pretty. I'm going to have my own work cut out to keep up with you."

Looking at her as she stood in the shadows beyond the narrow beam of light he thought he saw her flush.

She said: "Thank you. Dai left most of this side of things to me."

"I imagine I shall do the same," Charles said.

On the Sunday following his arrival, Charles proposed a run in his new Cat C gyro. After a momentary hesitancy, Sara gave way to his plea for a change of pace and scene. When the gyro lifted through the opened roof, it lifted into a clear sky. A cloud bank was visible, a white bar above the inland hills. Visibility was very good, and on the hills themselves small details stood out with surprising clarity. The gyro hovering, Charles pointed them out to Sara.

She said: "Yes, wonderful. Can't we run over there?"

He glanced at the electric battery indicator. "Just under a quarter. Any idea how far it is?"

She said vaguely: "Five miles. Ten?"

Charles laughed. "If it is ten, we'll probably have to walk part of the way back. All right?"

She smiled. "No objection."

He brought the gyro down on a grassed ledge about four hundred feet above sea-level, looking over the plain toward San Miguel, the laboratory, and the distant frieze of the ocean. The grass was short, probably sheep-cropped, but still wet from the storm; Charles threw a plastic sheet across it and they sat down. He began to offer her a cigarette, and then recollected himself.

"Of course, you don't. What do you take? Mesc?"

She shook her head. "No. Nothing."

"Nothing? Wonderful. You don't even bite your finger-nails?"

"Not even that. No credit, though. Remember my puritanical Siraqi upbringing. That accounts for it."

"I'd forgotten. Mesc and tobacco prohibited. You are allowed something, though. Is it—"

"You're probably thinking of wine." Sara was gazing out over the vista which lay before them.

Charles got up and went over to the gyro. "I have an idea—"

He fished in a locker and brought out two beakers and a couple of plasts of red wine. "Californian, I'm afraid. But better than nothing." He sliced the corner of one of the plasts and the wine gushed out into the beaker held beneath it. He handed it to Sara, and helped himself to the other. Tasting it, he said thoughtfully: "Not too bad."

"Here's to the solar battery," Sara said, "and we'll let our healths look after themselves."

She laughed. Watching her, Charles reflected that there was no trace now of the nervousness and awkwardness which had been such prominent features of her personality on their first meeting. And in their place, naturalness and charm were very prominent indeed. Especially the charm—he had a conviction of his own, growing all the time, that while it reflected the ease she had begun to feel in their companionship, it reflected something more, too; something that included provocation. Confident of not being unwelcome, he reached leisurely out to embrace her.

She pulled her body away, eluding him. Awkwardly he half-rolled, half-plunged after her, and managed to obtain an arm. To his astonishment, she slapped him sharply across the face with her free hand. He sat up and looked at her.

She began laughing, and broke off. "If you could only see how funny you look, Charles!"

"I can imagine it. What the devil—"

"You've forgotten. Another of our Siraqi inhibitions. Like cigarettes and mescalin. We find it very hard to be promiscuous at a moment's notice."

"How long notice do you require?"

"It's difficult to say. Long enough for you to be able to rule the idea out of your immediate calculations, at any rate. Shall we leave it at that?"

His face felt hot; he rubbed it. He was both annoyed and pleased. He had, in the past, deliberately chosen the Houses in preference to the promiscuity which was available about him, and had, on the whole, been willing to accept the popular view that this represented a perversity on his part. He was not so sure of that now.

"I suppose we must, if you say so."

"I've led a sheltered life. Remember, I've been with fellow-Siraqis all the time—first my father and then Dai. My opportunities have been limited."

"I'll try not to let them remain so."

"I suppose you will." She raised herself on one elbow, and pointed out to the gleaming fringe of sea. "Hydroplanes. It will be the return in the Guadalupe Chase. Have you any glasses in the locker, Charles? I've got a hundred on Conway."

He brought the glasses for her. "A good way of changing the subject. I gather you've got far enough into the swing to be willing to have a flutter on the hydroplane races."

She sat right up, straining her shoulders back as she focused the glasses on the distant specks in the ocean. The pose set her figure off extremely well; Charles had a suspicion that she knew this, too. The annoyance came back for a moment.

"They bet in Siraq, too. And they skip their hydroplanes better, incidentally. That's Ethelgar in the lead.

30

Conway's lying third. I shouldn't think any of them knows how to get the best out of a cross-wind."

"That isn't the Mediterranean."

"I told you—the Med is trickier than you people think." She lowered the glasses and handed them across to Charles. "Want to look? My hundred's gone. Conway's a good finisher but he'll never make up half a mile."

Charles took the glasses. "I've never been interested enough to bet on these affairs." He glanced casually through them. "I can't even make the colors out."

"You don't need to; the superstructure is enough identification. Look." She came over and took the glasses from him again. She rested her body against him, one of her elbows on his shoulder. He stayed quite still, aware of her warmth and softness. "Ethelgar—the high bows with the arched carapace. Conway—very low to the water and the wings slightly curved back. That's Spruce second; you can tell by the squareness."

She shifted away from him a little, lowering the glasses. He said: "Carry on. It's more fascinating than I thought. Who's lying fourth?"

She stood up, smiling. "Enough for one lesson, I think. You might find it too exciting. Shall we think of getting back?"

During the following week they had a couple of other outings together, and Charles was looking forward to the week end. He made some vague suggestion on the Thursday night when they were flying back from a trip to the Gulf. Sara shook her head; possibly regretfully, but very firmly.

"This is my Berkeley week. I go up to spend a couple of days with Daddy once a month. Sorry."

He was not sure whether he was disguising his disappointment. "Yes, of course."

She had told him she would be returning fairly late on Sunday evening, and he had put the gyro at her disposal. He still had the limousine and he got in some practice on it; having graduated to a motorist's status there was no sense in not acquiring the skill. Deliberately he stayed away from the laboratory for Sunday afternoon and evening. He hoped Sara would be back by the time he returned himself.

It was after twenty-three when he garaged the limousine, and he saw that there was no light from any of Sara's windows. She might have gone to bed as soon as she got back, of course, but it would be rather surprising if she had. He went to his own suite, but he did not feel like sleep. He buttoned Red League, Cosy Bright, and the local Sunshine Circuit. It was in the middle of this that he suddenly remembered there was a simple way of checking whether she had come back or not. He went out to the gyro shed. It was empty.

Everything seemed obvious now. There could be a hundred reasons why she should decide to stay with her father overnight and come back in the morning; he might be ill—anything. Charles went back to his suite, showered, went to bed, and slept until the trumpets of Cosy Bright woke him to a sight of an Alpine dawn sprawled across his bedroom wall.

He called Sara as soon as he was dressed. She herself had several times casually dropped in on him without warning, but he was not used to that kind of informality. The screen stayed blank. He let the call stay on for five minutes, in case she should be getting dressed or in the shower, and then accepted the fact that she still hadn't got back. He glanced at his finger-watch; it was past eight. Even if she had stayed overnight she should have got back by now, or at least called him up to explain why.

He found her father's frequency in his micro-file, and put the number on call. The call was accepted almost at once. The bronzed, typically Siraqi features of a man of about sixty—tall, a little stooped—came into focus. He had a friendly smile, but with a hint of slyness. He spoke with quite a pronounced accent. Presumably he had been a rebel himself from the tradition among aristocratic Siraqi families of speaking only French, since he had had Sara taught English from childhood.

He said: "Yes? You're Official Grayner. We haven't seen each other before. Wish you well."

There was a constriction at the back of Charles' throat. He said sharply:

"Is Sara—your daughter—there? I'd like to speak to her."

Professor Koupal's face tightened; he seemed to straighten fractionally. He said quietly:

"She left me yesterday—in the early evening—to go back to your laboratory. She has not arrived?"

"No." He was scared, and he rapped the questions out with involuntary sharpness. "Exactly what time did she leave? Did she say anything about stopping anywhere on the way? Did you notice the battery reading?"

"She left a little after six—eighteen, that is—she wanted to get back early, she told me. She said nothing about stopping anywhere—I told you—that she said she would get back early. The battery was charged. On the Saturday we had it charged, and we did not use it—the gyro." He paused. "What should one do, Official?"

"I'll get on to Telecom right away," Charles said. "Don't worry. She's probably had to ditch the gyro somewhere in the wilds. You can sleep in a gyro quite comfortably. I'll call you back as soon as I get hold of something."

He broke off without waiting for more than the beginning of Professor Koupal's reply: "Yes. I hope—" He got through to the Telecom Recovery Section. The screen showed a yawning fat woman, clearly interested in nothing but the arrival of the day relief shift.

He said brusquely: "UC Laboratory 719, San Miguel. Official Grayner. We have a member of staff missing. Assistant Sara Koupal. Missing between Berkeley and here last evening on a gyro flight. Have you anything in on her?"

She looked at him with bored and drooping eyes. "Almost swear not. Haven't had a gyro pickup in a month. Hold it, anyways. I'll check Field."

He watched her while she turned sideways and got

33

the Field group on another screen; he could just see a corner of that screen: a portion of a distorted male face. He could hear the reply she got, too. She flicked off, and came back to Charles.

"Nothing. I'll send it out on a rescue call. Berkeley, you said? To San Miguel?"

"Yes. You'll send a report in as soon as you get hold of something?"

She nodded. "You better flash her record-film to us, just in case. You got it there?"

"It's not here. I'll get it. I'll call you again."

"Do that."

She had turned away to watch the entertainment screen even before she broke contact. Charles stared at the faintly glowing screen for a moment or two before breaking contact himself. Then he went out to the office to find Sara's record-film. He brought it back to his living-suite. To check, he ran it through the projector. The particulars considered relevant to Assistant Sara Koupal filled the top half of the screen; on the lower half was projected Sara herself—three Saras: head-and-shoulders, front view and profile, and full figure. The fear, the pain, gripped him more sharply as he gazed at it.

He made the call to Telecom again, and the fat woman answered.

"You weren't long. Got the R.F.? Put it through."

The screen blanked for a minute or two while the automatic took over, photographing the record-film. Then the woman came through again.

"That's O.K." She smiled; a hint of malice. "Now I dig the rush. We'll try and locate her for you. It's a story for the telezine boys at that—beautiful girl scientist lost in gyro. You'll have them round fast."

Telecom always carried more weight than they were worth; Charles resented the woman but he kept the resentment to himself. In any case he must rely on Telecom for letting him have any news that came in promptly.

34

He said only: "We're restricted. Would you tell them that?"

"Never mind. They'll de-restrict you. You under Mettrill? They'll make him unlock."

He said: "Please let me have anything that comes in as soon as it does, will you."

As she said: "Surely," he switched off.

His next call was to Mettrill; it was a necessary notification. He had been through to Mettrill only once before; a formal call on his taking over the laboratory. Mettrill was the avuncular type—slow, friendly, eager-to-help surface, masking, Charles was sure, a typical file-and-forget lazy mind. This news made him sit up, though, and look irritated. It was something that was going to demand action.

Mettrill said: "You checked with her father?"

"Yes. She left with a full battery, just after eighteen."

Mettrill looked at him thoughtfully. "How did she come to be using a gyro?"

"I loaned her mine."

"Why?"

"I wasn't using it—to save her trouble. Otherwise it would have meant a taxi into San Diego and meeting the air schedules and the rest of it. She's a qualified flyer."

"Was, anyway." It was the casualness rather than the finality of the remark that made Charles want to hit him. "I advise you to stick to regulations, Official Grayner. It saves everybody trouble in the end, even if it means a little extra trouble in the short run."

"Yes."

Mettrill stirred in his chair. "What's her file number?"

Charles gave it to him. He watched Mettrill scrawl it down. He said: "I was wondering . . ."

Mettrill said: "Yes?" without looking up.

". . . If I could have another gyro sent up. I thought I might go out and have a look for her myself."

Mettrill looked up now. He fixed his gaze thoughtfully on Charles.

"We'll see about the gyro replacement. But stay where you are. Contact will have to drop in on you."

"I could make an appointment for them and still have time—"

"Stay where you are. You have work to do. We'll see about the gyro replacement—the other replacement, too."

"The other replacement" could only refer to Sara. Charles said, with a rising of anger: "Won't you at least say: 'But we hope it won't be necessary?' "

Mettrill continued to stare at him. "Two-thirds of the direct route between your place and Berkeley is over the ocean. I don't see any point whatsover in making your suggested addition to my original remark. Stay on hand, Official Grayner. Contact will be seeing you."

Mettrill's hand came forward to break, and then stopped. "And don't get in touch with anyone else about this. Telecom, for instance."

Charles tightened his lips. "The first call I made after hearing from Professor Cohn was to Telecom, to see if she had been picked up."

Mettrill leaned back and clasped his hands behind his balding head. For a moment he was silent. Then he said:

"When I was a young man, I did one thing thoroughly. I learned the regulations. It was the most useful thing I ever did, and I suggest it's not too late for you to do the same. Under 29 you will find a stipulation—no one—Supervisor, Official, Manager or Director—will communicate anything concerning managerial personnel to any outside source until after the matter has been referred to the next higher authority within the managerial. Words to that effect. There's always a reason for the regulations."

"This might have been a matter of life and death."

Mettrill glanced away. "I'll note that as your excuse. What did you get at Telecom—Recovery?"

"Yes." He didn't give a damn, at that moment, about anything except savaging Mettrill. "They had Assistant Koupal's record-film. I gathered they were putting it

36

through to TV. I informed them this place was restricted. They were going to contact you."

"Official Grayner," Mettrill said, "you're an incompetent fool. I'm breaking off. Stay where you are."

Charles put his callscreen on alarm before he went out. He went to the laboratory first. Luke and Tony were on some routine work Sara had put in hand. He told them what had happened. Then, not able to concentrate on the work he himself was supposed to be doing, he went outside. It was a gray sullen day, with a sharp damp wind coming in off the sea. He walked slowly down the path to the shore. Although remaining within earshot of the callscreen alarm, he was out of the noise range of the generators. It was very quiet. There was no sound but that of the sea, washing without haste against the rocks.

A hectic three days later Charles Grayner, waiting in Professor Koupal's Berkeley apartment, received permission to see his former manager, Ledbetter. Permission had been granted by Caston and Stenner, the two officials from Contact Section who had been assigned to investigate Sara's disappearance. As far as those two worthies were concerned, they had constructed a closed case for suicide on Sara's part; they had theorized she had never recovered from Humayan's death—she had never really been persuaded that he had not been murdered. Sara's father, whom Charles never got to see in the flesh, had also, according to Caston and Stenner, committed suicide—having left a note indicating he intended to do so, feeling that there was nothing left for him to live for after he presumed that his daughter had taken her own life. Charles, however, was unconvinced. Not only had the bodies not been found, though every means had been taken to locate them, without an iota of success, but there had been a curious something left by Sara which had not been satisfactorily explained—before she had disappeared, she had put in her fingerwatch to be re-charged. But Charles was not sure that he was going to underline this fact to Ledbetter. He did intend, he thought, to stand by his conviction that Koupal and his daughter had been kidnaped.

Charles took the Detroit stratoliner, and was there by eleven. He took a gyro-taxi direct to the UC building, and made himself known at Inquiries. The girl looked at her record board.

"Official Grayner? For the Manager. You're to go down right away."

Ledbetter rose to meet him as he entered the room, waved him to a chair, and said: "Well, for such a short stay, you've managed to run into plenty of trouble."

"A certain amount of death and vanishment."

Ledbetter looked startled. "What? Oh, I see. No, I wasn't thinking of that." He held up a couple of reports. "I meant these. 'Failure to comply with Regulations twenty-nine (iii) and forty-two (vii). Breach of Regulation twenty-nine (ix). Unnecessary invocation of Regulation one hundred and twelve (i).' Shall I translate? You notified the fact of your assistant being missing to an outside source before getting in touch with Mettrill, after previously giving her the use of your gyro, again without higher confirmation. You left your lab without getting in touch with Mettrill. And you insisted on by-passing Mettrill to give me your views on the situation, a course which is only justifiable in Regulations when a real suspicion of victimization can be established."

Ledbetter put down the reports and looked at Charles across the desk. His face was expressionless.

"There's another report from Contact which refers to your mental attitude; I gather that at least some of this has already been explained to you."

Ledbetter paused; there was an obvious implication that Charles should launch into some kind of explanation or defense. He refused the chance, and remained silent. Ledbetter gave him a little longer, while he tossed the reports back into his file tray. Then his blank expression broke, and he grinned.

"I told you you would like Mettrill. No reason why

38

you two shouldn't have got on together, except that a minor crisis blew up. Mettrill isn't good in a crisis. You did the right thing in coming to me. I can sort this lot out fairly easily."

Ledbetter leaned back and looked at his cigarette. "It's the future we have to consider. I'm not promising anything, but there's a chance I may be able to swing something useful there."

Charles said: "Useful?"

"It's a little out of the ordinary, but there's a chance I may be able to acquire extraterritorial rights in your Pacific Coast place. That would make you directly answerable to me for admin—reports would go through to Nikko-Tsi, of course, as before." Ledbetter grinned again. "There's an incidental advantage—I could use that tie-up for the odd trip to see you out there, and get a little yachting in. Well? How does it strike you?"

Charles said: "Favorably. You're being very helpful. But it wasn't precisely my future that I came to talk about—my future in that sense, anyway."

"No?" Ledbetter said. "All right. I've had Stenner's report. I've got some of it. You might as well let me have the rest."

Charles went through it for him, carefully and slowly, detailing Sara's original dissatisfaction with the result of the inquiry on Humayun's supposed death, and his own growing awareness that something was wrong with the superficial appearances of Sara's own disappearance and her father's suicide. When he had finished, Ledbetter commented: "That's all?"

"That's all."

"Now I've heard your interpretation of the facts. Will you take me as impartial?"

Charles said warily: "I've no reason to suspect you of not being impartial."

"I've thought a good deal about this. I had Stenner's report in last night; as you may guess, he mentions your theory only to damn it. That's a thing that always gets my back up. I began with a prejudice in favor of your

39

views. The case you have just stated would have confirmed that."

Charles caught at a phrase. "Would have confirmed it?"

Ledbetter nodded. "There are some inconsistencies in your theory. I imagine Stenner has pointed them out already. The odd time intervals between the 'kidnapings,' especially in relation to the Koupal girl and her father. The failure to take Humayun and the girl at the same time, presuming they were both 'wanted.' But those are mechanical objections, and I don't propose making them.

"No, it's the picture as a whole that I'm inclined to accept or reject, and I find it very difficult to accept it. You say that your predecessor, your assistant and her father have been abducted by Contact Section or some other managerial. My automatic reaction is to look for motive. If it were true it would represent a large-scale measure in any managerial's terms. Then, why? What reason could there be that would justify the risks involved?"

Charles studied Ledbetter closely. His lanky form was stretched back now in his chair, and he looked entirely and genuinely curious as to the answer to his question.

Charles said: "When I was here before, you seemed very uncertain as to the kind of work I would be called on to do at the new place. Are you still as uncertain?"

"It's interesting you should say that. Naturally the report from Stenner made me curious about the set-up. I sent a flip to Nikko-Tsi. I explained the situation briefly, and put a question to him: could I be told what work it was Humayun had been doing and which you were to continue—or if the information was top restricted, could I pass you on to Graz for their handling as I did not feel I would be competent to handle things myself. I had the reply printed. Would you care to see it?"

Charles nodded. Ledbetter brought out a sheet of paper, and passed it across the desk. Charles took it. It ran:

REFERENCE LABORATORY 719, SAN MIGUEL. ESTAB-
LISHMENT ENGAGED ON ROUTINE WORK INTO POSSI-
BILITY OF NEW POWER SOURCE CONNECTED WITH
IRRADIATED DIAMOND. RESTRICTED ON BASIS OF
INITIAL REPORTS FROM HUMAYUN. SUBSEQUENT
REPORTS HAVE NOT DEVELOPED PROMISE OF FIRST.
QUESTION OF CONTINUANCE OR RE-ROUTING OF THIS
RESEARCH WILL COME UP AT NEXT APPROPRIATE COUN-
CIL MEETING. GRAYNER TO BE RETURNED TO POST
PENDING FULL CONSIDERATION OF POSITION. YOUR
DISCRETION TO HANDLE. NIKKO-TSI FOR PRESTON.

Charles read the message through two or three times,
while he collected his thoughts. "Subsequent reports have
not developed promise of first." Something was wrong;
badly wrong. There were three possibilities. That Humayun had somehow, for some reason, not submitted
correct reports to Graz. That Graz was engaged in some
tortuous course of deceit which involved putting one of
their own Managers off the scent. Or that the flip from
Nikko-Tsi was a private forgery of Ledbetter's. The
second possibility seemed much the most likely. In any
case, since two out of the three possibilities involved
trickery within United Chemicals, the obvious thing for
him to do was to watch his step. He pushed the message
back to Ledbetter.

Ledbetter said: "Well?"

And something else was wrong. Ledbetter was too
amiable, too anxious *not* to embarrass him. He tried fit-
ting himself into Ledbetter's position, an imaginative
exercise more difficult for him than it would have been
for many others, because so infrequently practiced. Ledbetter had wondered whether there might not be some
truth in his suspicions, and had got in touch with Graz—
with the clear intention of ducking the problem should
it offer any major difficulties. Having got this kind of
reply it was reasonable enough that he should have re-
jected Charles' theory, but surely there was another implication to be drawn as well? Immediately before

Ledbetter showed him the message from Graz, Charles had referred to the work of the laboratory in veiled but portentous terms. Ledbetter had known—on the basis of his information—that there could be nothing in such a claim. His obvious move should be to put a disaffected and self-important subordinate in his place. Instead, he was watching Charles with friendly sympathy.

Charles said, striving to be noncommittal: "The flip seems clear enough. Your view then is—"

Ledbetter shrugged. "You've seen something of one of the missing three, so you're at an advantage there. But in my experience human beings can be very deceptive in that respect. I prefer to stick to the big picture. And that takes me back to the original question—what reason could there be to justify the kind of thing you have suggested? I'm not blinking the fact that there are several managerials who would stick at very little if they thought there really was something that would give them the advantage. I haven't forgotten the little shot Atomics had at—shall we say, centralization?—a few years ago. Or the Hydroponics—Agriculture combination in the 'Thirty-six famine. But what is there in this for anyone? Can you see anything?"

The solicitude was wrong, altogether wrong. There was one possibility, he reflected wrily, that might account for it. Stenner seemed to have had some doubts as to his mental balance. It might be that Ledbetter had them, to an even greater degree. Some people were naturally polite and considerate to the insane.

Temporizing, he said: "I suppose you must be right." He hesitated, summoning up words that would deceive the tall friendly man opposite him. "I won't conceal the fact that my assistant—Sara Koupal—made a very great impression on me." He smiled. "I couldn't conceal it, anyway, could I? It's in Stenner's report. There is no doubt in my mind that I love her. I found it hard to recognize that she might be dead; harder that her death had been of her own volition." He looked at Ledbetter, his embarrassment producing a good effect of honesty. "I still do."

"Naturally you do," Ledbetter said. "I don't think we need to call in Stenner's amateur psychoanalysis. Whether the affections are conditioned or free, one feels them—and damned painfully at times. This has been a bad business, even if an innocent one. Of course you would be inclined to see things the way you did. Anyone would. And it can't be much consolation to you now to be told that you will get over it—though you will. Work is a useful thing in that respect. I hope the flip I showed you won't put off the work, just because it hints at the possibility of things being changed. Actually, they will probably carry on under their inertia; you would be surprised if you knew some of the lines of research that have been automatically O.K.'d, year after year."

Charles said: "You want me to go back to the lab?"

Ledbetter said: "I'm pretty sure I can swing you under my jurisdiction. Mettrill is not the kind to stand on a question of prestige if he sees a chance of less work or less trouble. You will be O.K."

"Stenner's advice," Charles said, "was to visit Psycho and Med. He went so far as to suggest the prescription, too—a high-mesc course and a holiday trip."

"You can disregard Stenner. You are as sane as he is, and considerably more intelligent."

"As a matter of fact, I don't find the suggestion altogether repulsive. I could do without the mesc, but there is something about the holiday trip that appeals."

Ledbetter said emphatically: "Take my advice—work is the best remedy. A holiday trip is no good except to a mind already contented. You've got to learn to live with things. Work provides the best way of doing that."

There was an emphasis behind his words which it was difficult to believe stemmed entirely from his concern for Charles. Ledbetter wanted him back at the lab.

Charles said: "I guess it takes different people different ways. I'm not sure that it takes me that way. I

43

have an idea a holiday trip would be quite attractive." He glanced across at Ledbetter. "The change of scene, for one thing. The lab has acquired a few memories even in so short a time."

"Face them," Ledbetter said. "It's the only way to get on top of them; they would hit you with much more force when you finally got back."

"But then," Charles said, "I would be better able to cope with them. Or so I think. I take it there wouldn't be any actual *objection* to my consulting P and M and asking for the break?"

Ledbetter said, with obvious reluctance: "No. Of course you can. How long had you thought of asking for?"

"I hadn't thought. But with my grade and record, and with Stenner's report, I think I could probably get six months if I asked, don't you? And it happens that I have another six months' holiday furlough to my credit. I could take a year off."

Ledbetter was startled. "A year? What about the work?"

Charles shrugged. "It doesn't seem to have any urgency, as you and Nikko-Tsi have both pointed out." Ledbetter looked as though he were going to say something, and then thought better of it. Charles let a pause rest between them, to encourage him, but without effect. Then he relented. "I don't imagine I should want anything like that time, though. I've never had much pleasure out of furloughs in the past, and I don't suppose this will be any exception."

Ledbetter looked as though he had just thought of something. He said brightly: "I hope you won't take too long, for personal reasons. I'm looking forward to your hospitality to let me get those yachting trips in."

The KF studio had at one time been a brewery; long low-ceilinged rooms were broken at intervals by peculiar vertical shafts. Charles found Dinkuhl watching the interior of Room 17 through the glass partition.

He touched his arm; Dinkuhl looked round.

"Charlie! I heard you'd joined a procession to the morgue."

Charles said: "I've come for some more of your excellent advice, Hiram. And for permission to listen in on your grapevine."

Dinkuhl performed his characteristic mocking grin. "Advice is something we always have available. As for the grapevine, I'm not so sure. Come on upstairs, anyway, and I'll get you a drink."

There were two comfortable chairs in the upstairs room. Dinkuhl directed him to one, and went across to a spindly top-heavy Welsh dresser that just about covered one wall. He opened up a cupboard.

"Take what comes?"

"Within reason." He watched Dinkuhl pour two glasses and bring them over, together with the bottle, on a tray. "Turnip and tomato again?"

Dinkuhl shook his head. "The real stuff. Plum brandy. Well now. How've you been missing KF?"

"To tell you the truth, I hadn't given it a thought."

"You're a lucky man." Dinkuhl let his nose rest for a moment against the edge of his glass. "Ah. That's a bad business you landed in."

"What do you know about it?"

"Nothing," Dinkuhl said blandly. "You tell me."

Charles told him. When he had finished, Dinkuhl replenished their glasses. Charles looked at him. "Well?"

"And your good friends in UC haven't quite succeeded in persuading you that you are a promising psychotic?" Dinkuhl asked.

"I had my doubts at times, but I have none now."

"Good boy. It has long been a fixed principle of mine to assume that the world around me was populated by mugs and fleecers; I never take any man's word unless I know he has an axe to grind, and know just what the axe is. Then I can make allowances."

"What axe have you got?"

"An interesting point. Two, principally—to further

45

anything that looks as though it may sabotage, in the least degree, the managerial world in which we live; and to save my own skin."

Charles grinned. "All right. I'll settle for them."

"Not yet you won't. First I have to justify my seditious attitude." He finished his own glass. "You're not drinking."

"Not at your pace. I don't think I need the justification. I'm more concerned with getting some advice."

Dinkuhl filled his own glass. "The advice can wait. It won't be of an order to require your urgent attention—urgent within the next half-hour at any rate. Why do I wish to destroy this world-wide fatherly society of managerials in whose bosom we live? Why indeed?"

Charles resigned himself to the situation. "Because the end is in sight—the end of KF?"

"Partly, partly. But a few other things as well. Tell me —what anniversary falls two years from now?"

"I don't know. Should I?"

"It's the anniversary of the War. What do you know about the War—about the way the society of today came into being? I'll ask you another question. Professor Koupal taught History at Berkeley, one of the very few academic institutions which provide tuition in that subject. How many students did he have?"

"Before his disappearance? Two."

"You surprise me. Yes. Two. I doubt if there are a score of students reading History in continental North America. Although you could not be expected to appreciate it, this is—historically speaking—an extraordinary state of affairs. Other decadent periods have misread and distorted the history of their origins; ours is the first to have succeeded in ignoring it altogether."

"Decadent?"

Dinkuhl sighed. "I hoped I shouldn't have to argue about that. You must have been viewing Red League. Man conquering the last barrier—twenty-first-century Man grasping for a new heritage among the Stars— Conquering the Chill Lunar Wastes. But tell me: how

46

long is it since the lunar base was established? You don't remember. It was there when you were a child. Perhaps you can remember when the last attempts were made at Mars and Venus? You should remember them."

Charles thought. "The Del Marro expedition—"

"Over twenty years ago." Dinkuhl glanced at him sardonically. "You were a young man, then, settling down into your niche at Saginaw. That was Mars. They had ruled Venus out ten years before that."

"The difficulties are very great."

"Not as great as they were for the first trip to the Moon. But in any case, we aren't trying any longer. The work has been abandoned. Not worth the risk."

"The Moon," Charles pointed out, "hasn't been worth it. Except possibly in terms of astronomical research."

"By which," Dinkuhl said, "you display yourself as a true child of your age. If you are going to calculate that kind of endeavor in terms of profit and loss, then you have failed before you start. No, that is decadence."

"All right," Charles said. "I see why you would like to put a bomb under it all."

Dinkuhl ignored him. "How did things get like this?" He reached for the bottle without pausing and refilled his own glass and—over his gestured protest—Charles'. "In the twentieth century they knew—those of them that could see any further than their noses—that they were heading for a crash. And they got it, of course. They got the lot—atom bombs, hydrogen bombs, breakdown, disease, famine. The world's dark age beginning anew.

"And yet, before they had even had time to attune themselves to the new conditions—while they were still eating each other in order to stay alive and not for any pleasure in the taste of human flesh—the breakdown was over. The incredible was happening, and a new society was rising, lifting itself, as far as they could see, by its own bootstraps.

"Even though people today have succeeded so well in obliterating the memory of their origins, it is generally remembered that Atomics was the first of the man-

47

agerials, the resurgent center about which the forces of reconstruction gathered. From Philadelphia the call went out, and across the world, after a brief hesitation, came the response.

"The fact is that communications had become so good that, short of wiping out every small center of population, civilization was bound to recover. And not even all the large centers were wiped out, though few escaped quite as happily as Philadelphia. Atomics provided the nucleus of the new grouping of society, and the other managerials grew up around them; under their wing. The obvious ones first—United Chemicals, Agriculture, Hydroponics, Lignin Industries, Telecom, Steel, Mining and the rest; and after them the secondaries: Psycho and Med, Genetics Division, Leisure Group, and so on. The Council of Managerials was set up and now, as you know, in theory all managerials are independent and equal and with full sovereign rights. A balance of power."

"One thing I've never understood," Charles said. "How did Siraq come to be left out?"

"The Siraqis had spent centuries clutching the idea of a deity-centered nation. The managerial world had nothing in it they could possibly prefer to the concept of a Blessed Land. They made good use of the interregnum to occupy the Near East, and after that they stayed put.

"Today their country is cultivated up to the hilt and for the time being they have caught up with their population increase. Now, unless I am badly mistaken, you will see them go ahead."

"With the aid and comfort of Channel KF?"

"That," said Dinkuhl, "is my problem." He paused in the act of filling the glasses again. "I had almost forgotten that you had a problem, too. Tell me, what objective precisely have you got in view?"

"I should like to establish to my own satisfaction that my view of the recent happenings is the right one. More to the point, I should like to find Sara Koupal and ask her to marry me."

"What's the situation about leave?"

"I've been to P and M. They've given me up to six months' leave, and a number of containers of mescalin which I tipped down a drain."

"What are you doing with the leave—officially?"

"A trip to the Pacific Islands."

"Got the tickets?"

Charles patted his notecase pocket.

"Hand them over." Dinkuhl took the transparent plastic envelope containing the small colored plastic cards. "I know someone who will quite enjoy this trip. I would go myself if I didn't have something else to do." He glanced at Charles. "It is important that the tickets should have been used, just in case someone inquires. Now then, we're ready. First to my place, for a little plastic make-up and then elsewhere."

Two hours later, Charles inspected himself in the long mirror in Dinkuhl's lounge. In place of his own features —pale, thin, with straight dark hair and, as he had always privately thought, an intellectual cast—he confronted someone with light auburn curly hair and fuller, high-colored cheeks.

Dinkuhl said complacently: "I believe in the satisfied customer; quite an improvement. That fill-in on the cheeks will go six months, but don't wash it too violently. You can wash the hair. I know a tailor who will pad you out suitably, and you'll look fine. How do you feel?"

"I don't know. Comfortable. I think I prefer my old self."

"Voice," Dinkuhl said. "Voice and bad taste we can't do anything about. All right, let's go."

III

THE GENETICS BRANCH OFFICE was a four-story building on the corner of Cadillac and 17th. Dinkuhl and Charles went through to the central shaft, and on the third floor found a private room; the legend stenciled on the door was Official Awkright. Official Awkright was a short sandy-haired man who had something of Dinkuhl's own temperamental appearance. He pressed a button and the door closed behind them. Only then did he grin at Dinkuhl.

"How's it go, Hiram?"

"Moderately. Very moderately. Burt, this is Charlie. Charlie Grayner as was; now Charlie Macintosh."

Awkright nodded. He put a hand out and Charles took it. "Glad to know you, Official Macintosh. I've heard about you, Charlie."

"How's it with you? Who's in the lead now—Nature or Genetics Division?"

"Our brilliant scientists have developed an anti-fertility factor that can be added to the local water supply. From what I've seen of the figures, there will be some deaths, but not above one or two per cent, and the majority among the women."

"A wonderfully humane measure." Dinkuhl glanced at Charles. "Don't you agree, Charles?"

Charles could not help being offended by the realization that Awkright was passing confidential information to two men from different managerials. It was impossible not to be affronted by this; he viewed Awkright with combined amazement and mistrust.

Dinkuhl, apparently sensing the trend of his thought, said to Awkright: "Charlie's a rebel by force of circumstance, not by nature. Your disloyalty worries him."

Awkright shook his head. "I thought you'd brought a convert. What did you bring him for, if it comes to that?"

"For his GD card, in the first place. You can do that!"

"I can." Awkright stared at Charles, examining him with attention. "It might be useful to know what he's going underground for." Directly to Charles, he said: "I hear you got an adverse report from Stenner—you want to avoid a discipline? If you're not the rebellious type, it might be better to take whatever they gave you. There are difficulties in creating and maintaining a new personality."

Dinkuhl spoke for him: "No, not to avoid a discipline. Charlie is still well regarded in these parts. In fact, they are keen on his getting back to work as soon as possible. Some of them are. Officially he's got six months' leave on medical grounds, and officially he's going to the South Pacific Islands. Here are the tickets." Dinkuhl tossed the little envelope over. "Can you get these used today?"

Awkright looked at them. "They're for tomorrow."

"I know. Get them used today. It would not surprise me if Manager Ledbetter found a way of canceling them by tomorrow."

Charles said: "Canceling them? Why?"

"It's not unknown for Psycho and Med to call cases back for review, even within twenty-four hours. They might change their minds and decide you are fit for duty."

"I'll do it today," Awkright said. "I still don't know why he wants to get away, though."

"It's a private matter," Dinkuhl said. "He wants to find Sara Koupal."

Awkright smiled. He said to Charles: "So they didn't convince you?"

"No," he said. "They didn't convince me." He hesitated. "I don't quite know how you people can help me. Apart from the new identity and so on. And I'm not even certain that the new identity is essential."

Awkright said: "Well, that can wait for a few hours."

51

To Dinkuhl, he continued: "Bring him along this evening, will you, Hiram? I'll have the card ready."

The gyro slipped down toward a typical Agricultural outpost, the cluster of squat buildings which one saw universally from the air. Detroit was twenty miles away. The land here was flat and empty; it was not an area scheduled for night as well as daylight operation. Everything seemed deserted.

When the gyro touched down, Dinkuhl checked Charles' move to get out. Instead he rolled the gyro along, on the ground, toward the largest of the buildings that faced them. As they reached it, the doors slid open and the gyro nudged its way inside.

Charles looked around. Full lights were on; the place looked like a gyrotaxi hanger—he counted a score of gyros before he gave up counting. Dinkuhl got out, and he followed him.

Dinkuhl said: "Fair gathering tonight."

"Am I to know what it is yet?"

"Follow me," Dinkuhl said. "All shall be made clear."

They went through another long shed packed with gyros, and from that, through a connecting corridor, to a third shed, more square in shape. The people from the gyros were here, sitting in rows of chairs but also standing, in overflow, behind them. At the far end of the room a rough dais had been put up. There was a table on it, and a man standing behind the table. He was not particularly unusual except that he was bearded —although that in itself was unusual enough. He was in full flow of rhetoric; Charles disregarded this for the moment while he surveyed the audience.

At first glance they, too, were a very ordinary assembly; they comprised a well-varied set of age-groups between early twenties and sixties. The first thing to surprise him was that badges of the different managerials were scattered indiscriminately among them—it was not a question of a bloc of Atomics, a bloc of Mining, and so on; they were entirely mixed. Then he noted their faces more carefully. One could read the everyday features that they must normally show, but they were clouded now by something else—a concentration, a passion, which he never remembered seeing anywhere. He looked back to the speaker: it was there, too, and in a more powerful and vivid form.

He listened to what the speaker was saying.

". . . for time must have a stop! What comfort do I give you? No comfort but that of knowing and being prepared. For the sky will brighten and day will be more terrible than any night. It will be flames that brighten the sky, and the flames will be the flames of hell!"

When he paused, Charles felt rather than heard the sigh of indrawn breath from his hearers. He began to speak more softly, his words carefully brought out and speciously reasonable.

"Why do you come here, my friends? Why do you leave those airfoam seats in the cinemas, that TV screen, the airsphering and the lascivious picnics? Why do you leave all those pleasures and come here, to listen to me, a poor prophet of the Last Word that shall be Spoken? My friends, you come because you are in Hell! All that is necessary is that your eyes should be opened to see where you are and what your sufferings are to be. And Jehovah shall cause them to be opened! The hour must strike!"

Dinkuhl touched Charles lightly on the shoulder. He spoke softly in his ear:

"Not getting carried away, I hope?"

Charles looked at him, aware that his gaze left the man on the dais with a kind of reluctance.

"What in hell is all this?" he asked.

Dinkuhl jerked his head. "This way."

He led the way to a side door, and whistled it open. It closed behind them, cutting off the vibrant eloquence in the hall they had left. They were in another corridor.

Dinkuhl said: "Didn't you know about the Cometeers? They believe that the Day of Judgment will come as the Comet approaches, and the end of the managerial so-

53

ciety. The big boys know about them, and think they're unimportant. And that suppressing them wouldn't help, anyway—in which they are certainly right. Meanwhile, they provide a useful cover."

Through a second door they passed into quite a small room. There were half a dozen people in it; Charles recognized Awkright. Dinkuhl introduced him to the rest; he was confused and failed to take in their names, but he noted that one was from Atomics, one from Steel, one from Mining, and the other two from minor managerials—Psycho and Med and Interplanetary.

Awkright said: "You managed to get him here O.K.? The wanted man?"

Charles said: "Wanted?" Dinkuhl said: "Already?"

"The alarm went out late this afternoon. We got our own man through on to the Tonga stratoliner, but only just in time."

Dinkuhl said quickly: "Checking through to Tonga?"

"We've had the message mislaid for the night. It will get through in the morning. He will have got clear on a hydroplane before they can do anything about it. After that . . ." Awkright shrugged. ". . . There are a lot of islands in those parts, and plenty of places where a man who doesn't want company can hole up. With the help of a few wrong clues it should be a couple of months before they even suspect they're not going to find him."

Dinkuhl said: "That's all very satisfactory. Charlie boy, there's nothing to stop you going ahead with your plans."

"Nothing," Charles said. "Except that you haven't told me what they are yet."

Dinkuhl grinned. "Slack of me."

Charles looked round the little group. "I would feel a lot more at ease if I had some idea of what the whole gang of you were up to."

The man with the Atomics badge—Blain or Baines?—was a lean sardonic individual. He spoke in an English drawl:

"Hiram should have introduced us collectively as well

54

as one by one. This is the Society of Individualists, Charles, Headquarters Branch and General Assembly combined. We lift our helping hands to any little lame dog that looks like he's having trouble with his climbing apparatus. We don't amount to nothing, but we like to think we do."

Charles shook his head. "I still don't get it. But, I'll take it on trust for now. What do you want me to do?"

Dinkuhl said: "It's your angle from which we are looking at things. You want Sara Koupal. You have come to the conclusion—and it is our considered view that you are very possibly right—that she did not commit suicide or get herself killed by accident, but that she, and probably her father and Humayun as well, were picked up by someone for some reason not unconnected with the kind of work that was being done at your laboratory. Well, who picked her up, and where is she now?"

Dinkuhl gestered round the small room. "We have a fair selection here, as you can see. We hear a lot of things, but we don't hear everything, and whoever is holding these people will be exercising a certain amount of care in keeping the news from spreading. So the kidnaping could be the work of any one. Even Telecom. The point is that we have nothing to go on, as far as suspicion of some particular managerial is concerned. We all know Atomics made a bid for centralized control a few years ago. But Agriculture and Hydroponics had a try before that, and even innocent little Genetics Division have tried their hand—in their case a shot at producing super-geniuses who could do the rest of the work for them. In this case it might even be United Chemicals who had kidnaped their own people, though I can't think why they should—or why they should let Charlie here loose even for a few hours if they had done.

"O.K., I'll come to it. In my view, the only thing to do is try picking up the trail where the last scent showed. That means going back to Berkeley."

Charles said: "I stayed the night in Professor Koupal's suite. I went over it pretty thoroughly; so did Caston and Stenner. I doubt if anything will turn up there."

"There's more to Berkeley than Koupal's suite. There's his room at college. There's the chance that someone saw him in that crucial time immediately after he was last seen at the Interplanetary rocket pits."

One of the group objected: "Berkeley's not all that big a place, and everyone knows everyone in those campus towns. What excuse is Macintosh going to have for being there—he'll be noticed as a stranger, sure as H-bombs."

Charles felt a slight twitch of surprise at the use of his new name. It was used very casually; he hoped he would be able to use it as casually himself.

Dinkuhl said: "Charlie will have two authorizations along with his GD card. One will be a routine authorization of furlough. The other, specially fixed for the trip to Berkeley, will be an arrangement to stay over at Berkeley as a visiting student working on idiopathic decalcification in certain Outer Mongolian tribes. It so happens that they have some stuff on that at Berkeley that isn't available elsewhere on this continent."

Charles had started. "What," he asked, "is idiopathic decalcification in—"

"Their teeth drop out early," Dinkuhl said briefly. "We will hope you don't happen on another GD man working in that line—I think it unlikely. Anyway, that's the scheme. Once at Berkeley, it's up to you, Charlie. We'll try to keep in touch with you, but essentially you're on your own."

Charles nodded. The Atomics man said: "Sounds all right. I can think of about fifty things likely to go wrong."

"We'll hope they don't," Dinkuhl said. "All right, then. I'll run Charlie here back to Detroit and ship him on the stratoliner to Berkeley. See you boys at the next meeting."

The gyro dropped at last toward the lights of Detroit, and to Dinkuhl's house by the edge of the lake. Dinkuhl brought the vanes into vertical and switched on the landing light; the gyro dropped effortlessly on to its grounding strip.

Dinkuhl said: "I'll shove this in its kennel. You know your way about the house by now." He handed Charles the whistle-key. "Find yourself a drink. I'll be right up."

Dinkuhl had put on the path-lights; Charles walked along a narrow strip of light toward the dark house. He reached the door, and whistled it open; the inside lights went on automatically. He made his way up to the first floor, and into the lounge. There was a whiff of some kind of perfume in the air; it was oddly familiar.

He knew what it was when his knees began to buckle: astarate, the nerve gas. He slumped to the floor with his head toward the threshold—so it was that he saw Dinkuhl appear and stand on the other side of it, looking into the room. He was wishing he could read Dinkuhl's expression when consciousness went.

IV

THE CELL IN WHICH Charles awoke was windowless and approximately a cube, with sides of perhaps nine feet. There were two gratings facing each other in opposite walls—small square patches of mesh in a bare expanse of pastel yellow plastic. Ventilation ducts. A door was set in another wall. It was much too centrally placed; in point of fact the bottom of the door-frame was over a foot off the floor of the room, and there was the same gap between the lintel top and the ceiling.

Charles had a shattering headache; as he knew, an inevitable after-effect of astarate. He scrambled to his feet, wincing, and walked unsteadily across to the door. Dinkuhl's whistle-key had disappeared but he could remember a few standard combinations of notes. He tried them out, despite the dryness of his throat. There was no response; the door remained closed. He pressed his shoulder against it, too, but it remained firm. He went over and sat down in the airfoam chair to think things out. It folded persuasively about him, and he saw

57

that there were straps by which he could fasten himself in. He couldn't think why they should be needed.

He heard the usual mounting purr, and looked up to see the TV screen on the wall coming to life. A middle-aged man at a desk. A desk bare of anything that might identify it. And the man wore no managerial badge.

He was fat, red-faced, with a long thin nose and a remote sly look. He spoke with a slight lisp.

"How are you, Official Grayner? Is there anything you need?"

Charles said: "Yes. Water, a pain-killer, and an explanation. In that order, if it doesn't inconvenience you."

The man nodded. He called, to someone out of camera range: "Water and neurasp for Official Grayner." To Charles, he added: "You wouldn't prefer brandy?"

"Water will do."

"Let me introduce myself. My name is Ellecott."

"Of . . . ?"

Ellecot smiled; it was a dreamy unpleasant smile. "Don't think I want to be awkward. But I would prefer it if you did not press that question—not right at the moment."

The door opened. Charles went across and took a flask of water and two neurasp pills from a tall silent man, again unidentifiable as to managerial. He nodded to the figure in the screen. "Excuse me." While he was taking the pills and drinking from the flask, the door closed again.

There was an almost immediate lifting of pain. Feeling a great deal more comfortable, Charles dragged the chair over to a position more directly facing the screen, and sat down.

"You were saying?"

Ellecott said: "Simply expressing a hope that you would not object to my retaining my incognito. In a delicate matter like this . . . I'm sure you'll understand."

"I want to see Dinkuhl," Charles said.

Ellecott shrugged. "And if we haven't got him?"

"Then get him. He was standing just outside the door

58

when I passed out. I can't believe you would have left him behind to use the story on KF."

Ellecott shook his head with what seemed to be an attempt at roguishness. "We'll have to see what we can do. I don't know what's happened about Dinkuhl, but I'll try to find out for you. Like to have TV while you wait? You must find it boring in there."

There was one way of checking whether he was still on the North American continent, although he had no reason to think he wasn't. He said casually:

"Thank you. Red League will do. Unless you can get me KF?"

"I *believe*," Ellecott said, "that KF is temporarily off transmission. Red League coming up."

It was on the cards that Ellecott was telling the truth about KF—it was so much a one-man affair that Dinkuhl's absence for more than twelve hours would probably knock it out. But in any case they would hardly have been likely to give him information that would tell him explicitly that he was or was not in the Detroit area. He found himself watching some sort of ceremony. On the screen serried ranks of men stood on a wide expanse of parade ground. At signals, blocks broke away and marched forward to salute the UC flag. That told him the date—November 21st. Graduation day. He watched the marching squads with something of nostalgia, something of pity. With the aid of Psycho and Med, their minds had been sifted, their psychoplans prepared. And so they advanced—Squads A and B destined for leadership, the administrators and rulers of the future—Squads C, D and E for research and development work—Squads F, G, H and I for foremen and generally supervisory jobs—and at the end all those other squads who were now embarking on an adult life of routine and security and Cosy Bright in steady doses. The workers. Charles watched the gaily-colored standard flap in a sharp northeasterly breeze. He had been a Squad D man. He wondered . . . Dinkuhl's view that the managerial world was breaking down . . . could the explanation lie somehow in these neat military formations and the billowing flag?

The screen clicked to emptiness, and then the emptiness gave way to Ellecott's face again. Ellecott was still smiling.

"Good news for you, Official Grayner. We've got Dinkuhl. We can arrange for you to be quartered with him for the period of your—for the period while we are fixing things up. We're putting you into rather more comfortable quarters, too. I imagine you will be finding your present place on the cramped side."

Charles said warily: "That's very good of you."

"Two of our men are coming along to collect you now. I know you will co-operate."

It was when, at the bidding of the two men, he climbed through the door into a peculiar tunnel-shaped passage that he realized what his surroundings were. The original cell, of course, should have put him on the track —the functional bareness, the door equidistant between floor and ceiling, the chair with straps and the hammock. Now the convoluting corridor, the evidence of bulkhead construction, and, above all, the handrails for maneuvering in non-gravity conditions, made things quite unmistakable. He was in a spaceship. A spaceship at rest, it was true, since gravity was the normal gravity, not the artificial variety, and there was nothing of the inevitable background vibration. But a spaceship nevertheless. He glanced at his two badgeless guardians with private satisfaction. So it was Interplanetary who had him.

He recognized the room into which he was shown as one of the messrooms, converted hastily for his own and Dinkuhl's accommodation. The fine seams in the walls were indicators of the presence of pop-out tables, and there was the hatch in one corner, through which food would normally arrive. The TV screens on facing walls were messroom style, too.

A certain amount of odd furniture had been brought in, including, he was surprised and pleased to see, a

60

bookcase. Dinkuhl was standing behind this with a book in his hand. He looked up when Charles came in, and waved.

"Glad to see you, Charlie. They've already written me off as a big-mouthed recalcitrant so I will begin with a word or two of warning. Those TV screens may be blank, but don't think they aren't registering. And I know enough about modern microphones to be able to assure you that if you or I whisper loud enough for the other to hear, we are whispering loud enough for our friends to listen, too. That being so, I think they should be warned that we are taking the reasonable precaution of not discussing anything that in our view is likely to help them in any way."

Charles said: "Fair enough. How did they get you, by the way?"

"Astarate—but a milder dose than you, I gather. At any rate I have been awake for a few hours, and I took it you were newly risen. They told me you had insisted on our being reunited before you answered any questions."

Charles watched Dinkuhl, trying to probe whatever might underlie the familiar sardonic friendliness. "I thought it a good idea."

Dinkuhl nodded. "Very sound. I can't say what they planned to do with me—I was presumably picked up in the first place because I could hardly be left behind in the circumstances. But I take it I am dispensable. And that is something else that I think we must have out in the open, where we can see it as well as the eyes that watch, the ears that harken. To what extent are you to trust me? The fact that you asked to see me doesn't signify, except insofar as it makes things easier for them —supposing I am on their side."

Charles grinned. "The company is welcome, anyway. You restore my morale, Hiram."

"And that, too, can work both ways. But this seems a good time to tackle a point that I imagine may have begun to worry you—the question of your own impor-

61

tance. You will have realized that quite a number of people are more interested than a little in the work that was being done at the UC laboratory where you had so short and eventful a stay. Humayun and the Koupals may not have been captured by the same managerial. There is no reason to assume they were, and if they weren't, some of the apparent confusion in leaving Sara Koupal for a fortnight after Humayun's apparent death is removed. Now, is there anything that still strikes you as odd?"

Charles hesitated. Then: "The lab wasn't particularly well protected. All Humayun's reports were on file there. I admit I was a bit confused at first, but as soon as Sara explained what Humayun had been after, the pieces clicked together. Now these people who are showing such an interst in the whole business—I take it they must know what it is they are interested in. So in that case, why not simply pick up the reports? Why grab me?"

"That," Dinkuhl said, "is, of course, the crux of the matter. Why are you important—important enough to be treated with such circumspection by your own managerial, to be offered substantial aid and comfort by my own little group of subversives, and now to find yourself benevolently but firmly held as a prisoner by Interplanetary? The answer is: Your mind and its skills."

"I'm afraid that's nonsense. Sixteen years of a routine lab job don't make for indispensability. And it isn't as though the problem is a particularly stiff one. I can't see it offering insurmountable difficulties to anyone."

"Point one," Dinkuhl said. "The sixteen years were an error. I'll come back to that in a minute. Point two. I could show you a neat little problem in mike and camera handling which would leave you blank and wondering. It's not an exceptionally difficult problem, but you wouldn't get to first base on it, because you haven't got the basic orientation. Problems look easy to those who can see a way of cracking them; if you haven't the right kind of mind and the right kind of background, they're insuperable."

Charles said tolerantly: "And I'm the blue-eyed boy—the only one who can crack the nut? An odd coincidence that there should have been three of us linked together—Humayun and Sara and myself."

"Humayun and Sara Koupal," Dinkuhl said, "were Siraqis. In a way it was a coincidence that you should have been sent to take Humayun's place, but the coincidence was a limited one only. Now we come back to the question of those sixteen years in routine research at Saginaw. The coincidence was that after P and M had made their blunder and routed you into D Squad at graduation—what a lot we all know about you, Charlie! —you should have been shoved, entirely by chance, into work on the substance, diamond, that Humayun was going to do big things with fifteen years later."

Dinkuhl glanced at him speculatively. "I wonder why you didn't do anything big yourself?"

Charles said: "My procedure was mapped out for me. As far as I can see, Humayun was given a free hand. It's the only way you can hope to get anything valuable done."

"And, apart from Humayun, do you know of anyone who has been given a free hand in research?"

"I only know Saginaw. There were no free hands there."

"There are no free hands anywhere, Charlie. But it wouldn't matter a nickel if they were free, because they would not do anything. Yes, you might have done, but you were the exception—you were P and M's prize error. If your psychoplan had been properly prepared you wouldn't have been in research in the first place. You would have been fulfilling your rightful duties as an administrator. Along with Ledbetter and the rest of the boys."

Charles said: "I suppose so. You mean—"

"I've been trying to tell you for a long time," Dinkuhl said. "The managerial state is dead. And to a certain extent, killed by its merits. It evolved a neat system for picking out its better brains and giving them the plum jobs, but it broke its neck on a minor anomaly—that the plum jobs, whatever form of society you base your ideas on, are going to be the administrative jobs, the jobs involving power of men over men. Science doesn't fit into that capitalism, it developed a hierarchy which meshed in with the real society around it. Scientists did their good work while they were young, and landed the plum jobs in later life.

"But observe the managerial arrangements: a basic and largely disciplinary and conditioning training up to the point of graduation. Followed by specialization. Very efficient. Too efficient. Because to the managerial world it would seem pointless to train a man in the sciences unless he were going to spend the remainder of his life in those fields; and once he had been trained in a scientific discipline, then they made sure that he did that, and nothing else. You get it?"

Charles said: "And now they will have to do something about it—about science, anyway?"

"Now," Dinkuhl said, "they are doing only one thing—scrambling for the means of domination that's been tossed into the arena. What's the answer? One will get it, or more than one will get it. If the former, you have your centralized world control. If the latter, you either have a smaller, tighter hierarchy, or else a bloody struggle which one may win. Give managerialism credit for political astuteness—I think they will arrange it peaceably in the long run."

"And then?"

"Not much more than a century sees managerialism on the way out. I don't know what comes next. Maybe the deluge."

"But why destroy, without having anything to offer?"

"Some things need destroying. We should put them out of their misery." Dinkuhl smiled. "That's why I like you, Charlie. You're the kind of time-bomb they can't stop happening. You and Humayun and Sara Koupal."

"I can think of more comfortable roles to have."

Dinkuhl looked round for a moment, and then bent

down and stubbed his cigarette out against the TV screen control panel.

"Yes, you do have your personal situation to consider. Well, our Interplanetary friends, who have permitted me to get indignant at such length about the world at large, will presumably be coming through with a nice warm offer for you. You will understand that—could they be sure of knocking out Humayun and Sara Koupal as well—it might be more convenient for them simply to eliminate you. Shortsighted, but then, they are all incorrigibly myopic, as I have been trying to make clear. Well, they can't. At the moment, anyway."

Dinkuhl glanced thoughtfully in the direction of the TV screen on the near wall. "It would be more cheering, of course, if you could eliminate the possibility that the hierarchy will be formed *before* the weapon materializes. From their point of view—Interplanetary and whoever hold the remaining two—that might be a simpler solution. It must have occurred to them. In that case you would all become dispens—"

Dinkuhl broke off speaking. The TV screen was glowing into life. Dinkuhl chuckled.

"I thought that might fetch them."

Ellecott's expression, on the screen, was somewhat ruffled. He made an evident effort at self-control; the same thin smile on the same fat features.

He said: "I may say that my remarks, unless otherwise specified, will be addressed to you, Official Grayner. You wanted to see Dinkuhl again, and your wishes rank very high on our priority list. It is quite true that you are now in the hands of Interplanetary. You are of very great importance, not only to us in Interplanetary, but to the whole world."

"Where are Humayun and Sara Koupal?" Charles asked.

"We don't know—yet. We have a good Contact Section, and they are working on it. It will be a help when we have you safely at Luna City. We can then allow the rumor that we have you to get around. That may bring in something."

"I am not impressed by the prospect of Luna City," Charles said.

"Luna City is our stronghold. We could withdraw our relatively small bases on the planet and destroy every major city within twenty-four hours, from the space stations. It has never been considered."

Dinkuhl murmured: "I wonder if the fact that the other managerials keep Interplanetary's vital supplies on rather a hand-to-mouth basis could have anything to do with that?"

Ellecott ignored him. "We have long been perturbed by the trend of events, and we propose to use our influence to change them. But the immediate and urgent problem is the question of the diamond solar power-source. This can be used as a small portable but very powerful battery, as you know. It can also be used as a weapon, with some minor modifications. There are some managerials who would misuse such a power source and such a weapon. One of those may have either Humayun or Sara Koupal, or both. We need your help, Official Grayner, to enable us to keep abreast of this other, or others. With your help, we can maintain peace. Without it, there is the prospect of a confused and barbarous civil war, and perhaps at last of tyranny. As far as your future status is concerned, it is proposed to confirm you as a Director of this managerial, and a member of the Board. You will be given a free hand in your work, in the first place on Luna City but before too long, we hope, under your own choice of conditions here on Earth. Once the present crisis has been got under control you will be in charge of scientific development—and it is inevitable, you understand, that Interplanetary will have risen to a commanding position among managerials by that time. I think our offer is a fair one, and not unattractive. I hope you will agree to accept it."

"And if I don't?"

Ellecott smiled. "As an academic point, we'll consider that. You will still go to Luna City, of course, because in addition to our major concern of having you work for us, there is the minor concern of making sure you don't work for anyone else."

They didn't know where Sara was. Doubtless they would promise to get her if he were to co-operate; but they would be putting all their effort into the search for her and Humayun anyway, for their own purposes.

Charles hesitated. Presumably it was always a good principle to stall an unpromising situation. "Any reason why I shouldn't have time to consider things?"

"As long as you like," Ellecott said. He lifted his finger and looked at it. "Purely as a point of information, this ship blasts in three hours. But of course you will have the whole time of the journey to the Moon in which to think things over."

It was Ellecott's blandness as much as anything else which irritated Charles. They were not going to be budged from the path they had laid out for themselves. And they were certain that, in the end, he would come round.

He said curtly: "Never mind. I don't need time. The answer is no. I don't care for being forced into a membership."

Ellecott shook his head and shifted his glance. "Dinkuhl," he said "if I were you I should occupy the next few days in using your well-known arts of persuasion on your friend here. For both your sakes."

"If you were me," Dinkuhl said pleasantly, "you would spit in your eye, given the opportunity."

Ellecott was undisturbed, and said: "I propose leaving you alone now. You will be under surveillance, either by me or one of my assistants. You will have food and drink sent along shortly. Anything else?"

Charles patted the fuller cheeks which he now had. "There seems little point in my continuing to look like someone else. Can you send the fixings for Hiram to get these off me, and wash my hair back to normal?"

Ellecott laughed briefly, his voice rising approximately an octave when he did so.

"We'll have it done for you; we have a good cosmetics

staff. I'll send an escort to pick you up." He smiled. "*This* arrangement is permanent."

When Charles got back from having his make-up removed, Dinkuhl was watching TV. He switched the sound off, but left the pictures flickering on the wall.

Charles looked at his finger-watch. "We're due to blast in an hour and a half. I suppose Ellecott will come through and give us some final instructions before then. I don't even know how to fix those damned hammocks up."

"Blasting," Dinkuhl said thoughtfully. "I wonder how they will manage that? Tricky."

Charles echoed: "Tricky? What's tricky in it? It's a job they're used to."

Dinkuhl said: "Forget it. Sometimes my mind wanders. Yes, I think Ellecott will get through to us in the next ninety minutes. Meanwhile, let's make the most of things by seeing what Red League has to offer as a valedictory message from the planet Earth."

He switched the sound up. Then, oddly, the screen clicked off, and Ellecott's face appeared a few seconds later. He looked distraught.

"It's necessary to make some changes. Blasting will take place sooner than we expected; almost immediately, in fact. Get into your hammocks."

Charles shook his head. "We don't know how to rig them."

"I'll send someone down to—"

Charles and Dinkuhl saw Ellecott's face transfixed, the open mouth, the eyes staring, for some moments before his head slid forward to his desk. The screen showed the top of his head, with an incongruous bald spot in the center.

"Here we go again," Dinkuhl said.

"What the—"

"Don't talk. Take deep breaths. Keep on taking them. With astarate, the quicker you go out the less hangover you have later. I wonder who's got us now?"

68

PART TWO

V

FROM BEING AWARE OF the coolness of sheets and a background of muffled speech, Charles awoke more fully to the sound of a familiar voice.

Ledbetter was saying: "Yes, I think he's coming round now. Have you the neurasp ready, Nurse? Help me lift him up."

Raised into sitting position, he blinked in the bright glare of sunlight through plaspex walls. The nurse gave him the neurasp pills and he swallowed them with water. The pain began to ebb. He said to Ledbetter: "Dinkuhl?"

Ledbetter smiled. "Right beside you. He's not come out of it yet. I think there are signs of activity now, though. Neurasp again, Nurse."

Dinkuhl looked about him. "I'm still wondering . . . Ledbetter! Well, I'm damned!"

Ledbetter said: "I must apologize to both of you for putting you under with astarate, especially since I understand it was the second time in twenty-four hours. There wasn't any alternative, though. We had to act quickly."

"They were getting ready to blast ahead of time," Charles said. "I take it that means they were aware a rescue party was on the way."

"But not how far on the way it was," Ledbetter said. "Even the notorious Interplanetary efficiency doesn't always deliver the goods. We managed to get through and break a few astarate capsules into the air intake. Not before time. If they were getting ready to blast they would have been going on to internal air control at any moment."

Dinkuhl was staring at Ledbetter with a puzzled expression on his face. Ledbetter caught sight of it.

"Something bothering you?"

Dinkuhl hesitated, and then grinned and shook his head. "I guess my brain's taken a beating from those two helpings of astarate. What did you do with Ellecott and the rest of the boys?"

"We left them. There are good reasons why we don't want to make an open issue of all this. I don't think they will want to, either."

"No," Dinkuhl said. "I suppose not."

"Where are we now, anyway?" Charles asked.

"Vermont. Place called Pasquin."

"Long way from Detroit," Dinkuhl observed.

"You slept the journey."

Charles had been looking out of the plaspex walls of the room they were in. The view gave onto an ornamental garden, with a lake and what looked like a waterfall away up on the left. Beyond the garden's edge the ground fell away to a wide valley, bearing the marks of Agriculture's careful husbandry. In the distance there were gently rolling hills.

"What kind of an establishment is this?" Charles asked. "It doesn't have much of the UC stamp about it."

"It *was* a Director's mansion. You will like the layout, I fancy. I do. Marble saucepans in the kitchen and gold spittoons in the lounge. All the hooey and whatzis. I hope you like it, anyway. You'll have to put up with it for some time."

Charles' relief at seeing Ledbetter and finding himself in the hands of his own managerial again had blinded him to the circumstances which had led up to his capture by Interplanetary. He remembered now.

He said mildly: "There was a matter of six months'

72

sick leave that is due to me. I feel I need it more than ever."

"Canceled." Ledbetter smiled. "You'll find this a real rest home. It's called The Cottage, by the way."

Charles said: "I was under the impression sick leave was not subject to cancellation. Regulation—I've forgotten the number."

"I haven't. But there's always a regulation which cancels the regulation. It's an academic point. If you were tested by P and M again I have an idea they might find you fit for duty. But I don't think we need bother with that. You broke one or two regulations yourself in this business of taking tickets for the South Pacific, and getting yourself fixed up with a new face and a GD card."

"Is that a threat?"

Ledbetter shook his head in mock despair. "For heaven's sake—we're not Interplanetary! You're home again, in UC. There's no need for threats, or anything else. You're amongst your own people."

Dinkuhl said: "Excuse me if I turn my back on this touching family scene."

Dinkuhl got up from his bed, and went across to the plaspex wall to get a clearer view of the grounds. He was wearing a night-smock, and Charles realized that he had been fitted into one, too, while he was unconscious.

Charles said: "I haven't noticed all that much of trust and honesty from my own people in the recent past. You weren't doing badly at persuading me the work Humayun and Sara had been doing—the work I was supposed to take over—was unimportant. And then—wham! I find myself important enough to be astarated twice in one day."

"All right, we tried to fool you," Ledbetter said. "But it was for your own good. Our judgment was that your peace of mind would best be secured if you could be made to believe that Sara was dead, and that you were simply to carry on a routine job which your superiors were too dumb to evaluate. We figured that you had already shown more than enough initiative in going after her, and we didn't see how we could keep you on the job —a vital job—if you thought there was anything to be gained in continuing the search. Meanwhile, of course, we had put Contact Section onto looking for her, her father and Humayun."

"Have you any clues yet?"

Ledbetter shook his head. "It's only been a couple of days, remember. You were never meant to have sick leave in the first place. I had to let you go to P and M to stall you, but we had already arranged for it to be canceled. That was a neat business with the tickets!"

Ledbetter's face broke into a lean smile.

Charles said: "I was wondering, a while back, how Interplanetary managed to get on to my tracks as easily as they did. The same applies to UC. How did you manage to pick up the trail?"

"Contact Sections," said Ledbetter, "are not always as inefficient as they generally seem. As for their methods, I'm afraid that's one regulation I have to take seriously myself—Regulation Seventy-three: Detailed information on Contact Section activities is most expressly secret and not to be divulged even within the managerial—even to a superior at the superior's request. You can just take it that anything Interplanetary can do, we can do better."

"Now you surprise me," Dinkuhl called from the other side of the room.

Ledbetter glanced in Dinkuhl's direction—he had his back to them—and winked at Charles. It was a wink designed to convey a lot: amusement and tolerance and complicity against someone who after all was not UC. A regular guy, but not UC. It was difficult not to respond to it. It was part, after all, of the entire difference of atmosphere, of the heart-felt relief—not only at being rescued and being spared Luna City, but also, more subtly, of being back: a confirmation that the world was not quite as bad as all that.

Charles grinned in return.

74

Dinkuhl came over and sat on the edge of his bed, his knees spread under his night-smock.

"Well," he remarked. "Have we got it on the deck now? Charlie is still the guest who mustn't leave? You wouldn't have a little lab fitted up for him out back?"

Ledbetter and Charles both laughed. Ledbetter said:

"It so happens . . . the stuff isn't here yet, but there's a good suite of rooms that can be used. The Director used to have a model layout of the old train systems in them. Very good light. We shall look after you, Charles."

It was the first time Ledbetter had used his given name. Charles was not disposed to think much about that because he was still too amazed by the fact that Ledbetter was treating what he had thought to be Dinkuhl's joke seriously.

Charles said: "You mean that? I'm not to go back to San Miguel?"

Ledbetter made a gesture of negation.

"But the idea was that I should go back there."

"Shall we put it this way?" Ledbetter said. "That this recent affair has given us something of a shock. Naturally we had woken up to the fact that some managerial or managerials had wanted the other two badly enough to take some trouble about getting hold of them. As a result we were prepared to have to look after you very very carefully indeed. But we now realize that we must be a lot more careful even than we had planned. San Miguel is out. It would be like putting the honey back in the hollow tree once the bears had found it.

"So instead of San Miguel there's Pasquin. We think we have covered our tracks this time. There'll be ample guard on, just in case we haven't."

Dinkuhl smiled. "All right then, no complaints. You'll do one little thing for me?"

"Within reason and ability."

"I've got an assistant. No cap on that 'a.' He's not what I would pick for my successor, not by some distance, but he should be able to keep the flag flying for—for the duration I think you said? If I give you a message with some elementary instructions—mostly operating guff and so on—will you get it through to him for me?"

"Don't see why not. Provided it's in English."

"You set my anxious mind at rest," Dinkuhl said. "Now that I have done my duty, I guess I can take it easy. I don't land any chores here, do I?"

"No chores. I wouldn't mind the life."

"One little thing. So small it embarrasses me to mention it. I suffer mildly from satyriasis."

Ledbetter smiled. "See what we can do."

Dinkuhl raised his hand. "I'm not asking you to prostitute the virgins of United Chemicals. This is a horse that works for its feed, and likes it that way. Just so it isn't an exclusively male staff, I'll manage O.K."

"Set your mind at rest," Ledbetter said. "But right at rest. We shall do what we can to make this a happy and profitable stay for both of you. The only difference is that we shall expect Charles to do a little real work now and then."

"The ties of home," Dinkuhl said. "A homeless wanderer like me must sometimes think of them with a pang. Charlie now, looking cheerful about the prospect of sorting out his bag of tricks, for the glory of UC and the use of a gold spittoon. And a little while back he was spurning a Directorship."

"We put first things first," Ledbetter said. "The important thing is the job." He looked at Charles. "There will be a Directorship afterwards. You can take that for granted. Just now we've got to keep you here and under supervision, for reasons you appreciate as well as we do. You have already been promoted Manager, but it would be pointless to create you a Director until you can be one in fact as well as name. You see that?"

Charles nodded. It was odd, being told so casually of the Managership he had abandoned as out of reach more than ten years ago. Odd, and unimportant.

Dinkuhl said: "Whatever goldfish bowl they put you in, Charlie, you just bob right up to the top. Mind you don't pop right out of the water."

The words were as trivial-sounding as Dinkuhl's generally were, but Charles wondered whether there was not a little more edge to his voice. He wasn't going to worry over it, anyway.

Ledbetter said: "It's been quite a rush job, and I've got a few things to look after. You have a four-room suite here, with a sun-terrace leading from the next room. But that's just for your privacy—you are at liberty to roam all over The Cottage and the grounds; incidentally there's a very nice bar on the other side of the house. Well, that's that. We're getting the stuff through for the lab as quickly as possible, but it will take a few days. Take it easy till then." He paused slightly. "I hope you will be able to take it easy. We know how concerned you are over Sara. But you do realize, don't you, that by yourself you could never have hoped to rescue her? All you could do would be to put yourself in jeopardy of capture—as you did, of course.

"At least you know now that UC Contact Section is on the job, and I think it's as good a Contact Section as any you are likely to find. If anyone can get her, they will. And meanwhile you have the consolation of knowing that whoever has her will be looking after her. She is as valuable a piece of property to them as you were to Interplanetary."

Charles said: "I suppose so."

"An added incentive when we have the lab fitted up! The sooner this business is over, the sooner things get back to normal."

"Providing, of course," Dinkuhl said, "that as good a Contact Section as any you are likely to find doesn't turn the goods up even sooner."

"Exactly," Ledbetter said. He glanced from his finger-watch to Charles, including him again in that managerial warmth from which Dinkuhl, with all his many qualities, had excluded himself. "I must streak. Have a good time."

Charles walked on his own in the grounds some days

later. He was glad of the solitariness, and glad also to be away, for a time, from the centrally-heated Cottage and its sub-tropical roof-garden. The weather outside had turned sharply cold, and it was bracing to walk through the bare outdoor garden and into the scattered timber beyond. The deciduous trees were bare, of course, but there was a belt of evergreens to the north and east from which the house was completely hidden.

The main track from the house led through these evergreens to a massive gate in the barrier fence which, heavily wired and with the ground cleared for five yards on either side, stretched around the perimeter of the grounds. Charles stood for a while gazing curiously at the gate. It was a check-point; a guard in UC uniform nursed his Klaberg rifle inside a small sentry-box with a plastic bubble top. The small nozzle in the plastic, just above the box's waistline, would be the astarater: a touch from the guard's finger could blanket the area around in a few seconds.

Quite an adequate safeguard. Theoretically someone might shoot the guard through the plastic, but that would actuate an alarm system, touch off the astarate, and bring a gyro from the house almost as quickly. A situation that would be infuriating to someone anxious to escape; he was pleased that he was not in that frame of mind himself.

He watched the guard changed. The gyro side-slipped through the air from the roof of The Cottage, and dropped on to the track just inside the gate. The new guard got out and, after a word or two, the old guard took his place. The gyro climbed back to its eyrie through the damp wintry air. Informal but effective. Charles walked on, his footsteps deadened by pine needles.

As he reached the edge of a clearing among the pines, he heard a low whistle. He turned quickly. Dinkuhl was standing by the side of a tree, watching him. He beckoned Charles over.

Dinkuhl said: "Charlie boy, time is short. Come over here and sit down."

78

There was a fallen tree. They made themselves comfortable and Dinkuhl brought out cigarettes. They lit up. The smoke rose in straight plumes; it was cold but there was no wind this morning.

Dinkuhl said: "You happy here?"

"Tolerably." Charles glanced at him. "You seem to be."

"What's the difference between being held here and being held by Interplanetary—ruling out Luna City for the moment."

"That's a lot to rule out. Quite a difference."

The important difference—that here he was with his own managerial—was one it would have been embarrassing to put plainly to Dinkuhl.

Dinkuhl glanced at him, smiling a little. "Such as being in the bosom of United Chemicals?"

"I wouldn't rule that out. It's what I'm used to."

"And what makes you confident this is a UC set-up? That they wear the right badges?"

Charles looked at him in complete astonishment. He saw what Dinkuhl might be driving at, but it was a conception so fantastic as to be hardly within the bounds of sane speculation.

He said reasonably: "You forget something, Hiram. Ledbetter was my Manager at Detroit."

Dinkuhl nodded. "For your work in the lab here—you said you were going to ask Ledbetter for your old assistant from Saginaw. Did you ever do that?" Charles nodded. "And—"

"He wasn't available. Reasonable enough. Ledbetter told me they have a couple of good youngsters they're bringing over from Europe."

"So, apart from Ledbetter, there aren't any UC people here you can recognize?"

"It isn't likely there would be. They're mostly Contact Section, after all."

Dinkuhl wrinkled the top of his head. "Let that go. Where would you say we were before Ledbetter and the boys launched their Men of the Mounties rescue stunt?"

Whatever harebrained notion Dinkuhl had got hold

of, the sensible way of treating it, Charles recognized, was to meet his points logically and sensibly. He said:

"In one of Interplanetary's spaceships—freighter, type seven, by your reckoning—in the Toledo pits."

Dinkuhl grinned. "Quite some Contact Section, as Ledbetter said. Breaking and entering the Toledo pits at a time when Interplanetary had their most treasured possession stowed away on a freighter there. But that wasn't what roused my suspicions. I told you when I first met you in that phoney messroom that we should keep quiet about everything that mattered. One of the things that mattered was that that freighter was wrong in small details. Minor things. They had pop-out tables, but they'd missed the pop-up ash-trays; I had to stub my cigarette on the TV control panel. And the corridors hadn't taken the battering all round that they get from use in free fall—the track was all worn on the floor. Something else, too. I'll come to that.

"Anyway, the thing to do was to string them along, whoever they might be, and wait for something else to happen. In due course, it did. United Chemicals to the rescue. Virtue triumphant."

Charles said: "It strikes me as crazy. I hope you don't mind my saying that. Why should UC—or whoever you think it is masquerading as UC—do something as complicated as that? And what about the offer Interplanetary made me? I might have accepted it—what then?"

"That puzzled me a little," Dinkuhl admitted. "I wondered how they would fake the take-off, and the space flight, and the lunar conditions. Not impossible, but very very tricky. But there was no real need for them to do so. Had you taken the offer, there was nothing to stop them changing their minds and keeping you on an Earth base; it's easy enough to think of adequate reasons. You were never meant to take the offer, of course: it was put simply to soften you up psychologically, to ensure you were properly grateful for being rescued. Even if you had taken the offer, the rescue

80

might still have taken place, for much the same reason.

"As for the complications, the people who pulled this job are not inartistic. They have you summed up as loyal to your managerial, and unlikely to be genuinely at ease under terms of constraint to any other. At the same time, you had shown signs of initiative and some rebelliousness, so if they put on the UC cloak at the beginning and clapped you in custody for your own good, you might very well be awkward about it. Their solution was good: have you captured by—as you thought— Interplanetary, and then rescued by—as it seemed— United Chemicals. Up goes loyalty and gratitude; down goes rebelliousness."

Thinking he saw a flaw, Charles said:

"The fact that the spaceship was a fake may show that it wasn't Interplanetary who had us at first, but it doesn't mean it wasn't UC—"

He broke off. Dinkuhl said: "It does, though, doesn't it? When I woke up and saw Ledbetter, I wondered. When I heard him talk about rescuing us from Interplanetary, I knew the play was still going on. If it had been a genuine business, he would have mentioned the name of the real villains."

"But what if the whole scheme you've outlined was planned by UC—for the reasons you gave, which would apply almost as well in that case as in the other?"

"Yours," Dinkuhl said, "was a simple-minded managerial, as managerials go. But in any case, I happen to know we are not now being run by UC. Come back to that. You didn't feel quite easy in your own mind, when you first woke up in The Cottage, did you?"

Charles said: "It didn't amount to much. As I recall, it was you that put me at ease again."

"I'm rather pleased with the way I've handled this." Dinkuhl smiled. "I have my vanity, difficult as it may be to observe it. But luck has run my way, too. The fact that I made such a business of warning you, on the spaceship, that the walls had eyes and ears, told in my favor when I carefully didn't warn you after Ledbetter and the boys picked us up. I played everything for the audience when I was talking to you. The safest man is the man who thinks he can see through things—so I let them see I thought I could. Like that spaceship being a seven freighter. This is the major league. No fooling."

Charles said slowly: "It's hard to believe that."

"If it were easy to believe it, they would have slipped up. And they don't slip up on atmospheres—they've had plenty of training in them."

There was a moment's silence. Then Charles said: "If they're not UC, who are they?"

Dinkuhl flicked the stub of his cigarette up into the gloomy branches of the firs.

"Who," he asked, "would be likely to have a mock-up of a spaceship? That was the big question. If not Interplanetary—who?"

"Go on. It doesn't mean anything to me."

"It did to me. Something else confirmed it—a certain kind of track, marking the surface both in the corridors and the messroom. I knew what caused that track. TV camera cables. It was a mock-up Telecom had built for shooting spaceship interiors for the space opera serials. I made my final check after we landed here. Remember I told Ledbetter I wanted to send a message through to my assistant on KF—technical advice? Ledbetter said yes without hesitating. He would have hesitated all right if he had been UC, because UC don't have anyone who knows enough about TV operational jargon to be sure I wasn't passing a message outside. Telecom do."

"Telecom," Charles said. "Well, I'm damned."

Dinkuhl grinned. "We both are. You'll soon see. It would take Telecom to have the kind of spy equipment this house has, too, incidentally."

Anger was beginning to replace confusion in Charles' mind. He said tightly to Dinkuhl:

"What are we going to do?"

Dinkuhl looked at him. "You're the H-bomb. The way I see it, you can do one of three things. You can go back and get on with the job for your new employers.

I see it, you can do one of three things. You can go back and refuse to get on with the job. I don't advise that. Ledbetter has plenty on the ball, and he's playing for big stakes, remember."

The confusion returned. Charles said:

"Ledbetter *was* UC. How does he come to be working for Telecom. I just don't get it."

"*Sancta simplicitas,*" Dinkuhl commented. "You wouldn't get it. I know a little about Ledbetter. He had a tough start—a background that would have been damn bad even in previous centuries. Both parents drunkards and fighting. He was a bright kid. He fought his way up to the top. But the top goes right up to the sky for that kind of climber. And managerial loyalty is only skin-deep, if that. No, George isn't the kind of playmate I recommend for you."

"The third thing. What was that?"

Dinkuhl eyed him steadily. "Escape."

Charles looked around. Through the trees the barrier fence was visible, rising to perhaps ten feet.

He said: "Easy. Which way do we do it? I throw you over first, and then you throw me over?"

Dinkuhl smiled. He consulted his wrist-watch again. "The time approacheth. Leave it to your Uncle Hiram."

"I'd prefer to have some idea of what you propose."

Dinkuhl took his arm. "We're going to borrow a gyro. There isn't time to explain everything right now. Down to the sentry-box. We've got a friend in the camp, though he doesn't know it yet." Dinkuhl had begun to walk down the wooded slope toward the gate, and Charles, automatically responding to the pressure on his arm, walked with him. "I told you—I never forget a face."

Charles could see the gate now, and the upright figure of the guard inside his plaspex bubble. Dinkuhl went on talking, in a slow drawl that might be concealing nervousness.

"I've had enough time thinking about this. It should go O.K. I thought maybe it would be rushing things to try it this morning, but my principle is that it's always safer to act at once, unless you can act sooner. If not now, we would have had to leave it till tomorrow afternoon. That's when our friend is on guard again."

They were approaching the sentry-box. Charles could see the tall immobile figure through the plaspex; he looked a very ordinary character, in UC uniform, with the UC badges. His eyes were fixed coldly on them as they approached.

"That was another thing," Dinkuhl said. "When I saw him before, he was wearing a Telecom badge. Though since his activities on that occasion would properly be classed as subversive, that wasn't conclusive in any way."

Dinkuhl tapped on the plaspex. The guard unseamed his sentry-box and came out toward them; he had his Klaberg at the ready and was wearing the nose filter against astarate—presumably the Klaberg was fitted with an astarate release.

He said, his voice midway between deference and challenge:

"Anything I can do for you?"

Dinkuhl looked at him for a moment. When he spoke it was with the full resonance of voice that he could muster up when he wanted to. He said:

"Brother, are you damned?"

The guard only looked surprised for a moment. When he spoke it was in a liturgical tone of voice matching Dinkuhl's own:

"Damned to Hell. Brethren, are ye damned?"

"Damned to Hell." Dinkuhl jerked his head toward Charles. "In this brother's mind, the Lord has planted power and a sword. He must be free to serve the Lord whose Finger lights the sky to destruction."

The guard inclined his head. "To the Damned all gates are open."

Dinkuhl looked at the gate—a little wistfully, Charles thought. It was a temptation simply to get out and trust to luck after that. Dinkuhl said slowly:

"We need a gyro, brother. Your relief will be along

inside five minutes. I wouldn't fit in your uniform, but this brother will. I want you to let him take it. We will tie you up. The Will of the Lord, brother."

The guard nodded. Without hesitation he stripped his equipment and his outer garments from him. In the sentry-box there was the usual plastic exudator. Dinkuhl adjusted the nozzle to quarter-inch orifice, and at a touch the plastic rope ribboned out. Carefully and deftly he tied it round the unresisting guard. Charles watched him while he was himself putting the uniform and accoutrements on.

Dinkuhl said: "You get the sticky job, brother Charles. The Lord didn't see fit to provide me with the figure for it. Club him with the Klaberg if he's wearing his nose filter. In fact, it will be safer to do that, anyway. There doesn't seem to be a spare filter here, and you would have an even stickier job carrying me if I passed out. Hit him hard, for God's sake. I'll be crouched in the box and I'll come a-running if you get into trouble, but it's always better to make sure at the start, if you can."

Charles felt tense; it was not an altogether unpleasant feeling. The prospect of doing something violent soothed that part of his mind which had been most outraged by Dinkuhl's explanation of the double trickery that had been practiced on him.

Dinkuhl completed the tying up, and propped the guard in one corner of his box. He pointed toward the distant house. A gyro was lifting from the roof.

"There's your quarry. I'm getting inside. Don't forget —hit him hard."

"Don't worry," Charles said.

He stood just outside the box, Klaberg held loosely, waiting for the gyro. It arrowed down through the wintry air, rotors flapping idly, and perched on the road perhaps ten yards away from him. The left-hand door slid open, and a figure dressed as he was dressed jumped down. It was a relief to observe that he was only of middle height.

He walked up to Charles. He said curiously:

"You're not Herriot."

Charles made an attempt at disguising his voice. He had his hood close round his face and was not seriously worried about his features being recognized.

He said: "Herriot went sick. Didn't they tell you?"

"Where you from?"

Charles ignored the question. He stooped down toward the base of the sentry-box, and poked at it with his Klaberg.

"You know the condition this was in? Somebody should have reported it before now."

He straightened up himself as the new man bent down to see what he was talking about. Behind the ear, he thought to himself. He didn't aim well enough, and the butt of the Klaberg landed at the base of the man's neck. He rolled over and lay slack.

Dinkuhl emerged from the sentry-box.

"Charlie," he remarked, "you're a man of action. I could not have done any better myself."

The man lay still. With rising nausea, Charles contemplated the possibility that he might have done the job too effectively.

He said: "I hope I haven't finished him off."

Dinkuhl knelt down. He said: "Fetch me a hank of rope. No, he'll live to explain to George what a sucker he's been. Should make it less tough for Brother in there. For suckers the only safety is in numbers."

When he had been adequately roped, the guard was pushed into the box with his companion. Dinkuhl led the way to the gyro. He clambered up through the open door and Charles followed him. Dinkuhl took the controls.

"Time," he observed, "is on anyone's side but ours. This is where we move."

The gyro climbed steeply, and headed north.

VI

THE ROLLING COUNTRYSIDE OF Vermont was spread two thousand feet beneath them. They were heading north.

Charles asked: "Montpelier?"

"Thereabouts."

But Montpelier came into view below and their course held. Dinkuhl was apparently in one of his moods of concentration; it was abundantly clear that he had his plans and did not want to discuss them. Charles assumed that he had changed the immediate objective to, possibly, Quebec, perhaps because their escape had gone so well so far. Quebec would give more scope for losing traces.

Montpelier was three or four miles behind them when the gyro started to come down. The country was bleak and empty here, and Charles' first thought was that the gyro might have developed a fault. But Dinkuhl was directing the descent. They landed in one of Agriculture's vast potato fields. At Dinkuhl's gesture, Charles jumped clear; his feet sank into the moist crumbling earth.

Dinkuhl came out on to the gyro's running-board, but did not immediately drop from it. He was apparently adjusting the controls. The gyro began to rise again, and Dinkuhl fell, landing on hands and feet. The gyro's door was still open as it disappeared on a continuation of its northerly line of flight.

Dinkuhl wiped his hands on the back of his trousers. He looked after the retreating gyro, and said happily:

"They gave us too much time. I don't mind confessing a certain relief."

"We were clear, anyway, weren't we?"

"That was Telecom we left. They have resources some other managerials don't. Their gyros can all be tracked from their control points." He laughed. "They can follow that now. Maybe they'll bring it down before it reaches the Hudson. But they will. They'll intercept from Montreal and Quebec." He looked around expansively. "We're clear, Charlie boy. I never really thought we'd make it."

Charles looked around himself. It was a field of a hundred acres or bigger. Beyond the distant wire fences there seemed to be other similar fields. The sky was low and trailing strands of dark cloud. It was the first time in his life he had been isolated in the country without a gyro or some similar form of transport, and the experience was a depressing one.

"Clear," he echoed. "Clear to do what?"

"To walk back to Montpelier." Dinkuhl grinned. "A healthy and invigorating exercise."

"And after that?"

"Gyro-taxi to Detroit. Then we'll see. Meanwhile, the invigorating walk."

Taking a southerly line, they trudged painfully across the ploughed field. They were nearing the first fence when Dinkuhl pointed to the sky. Two gyros were flying north. They stood and watched them until they were out of sight again. Then they climbed through the fence; another fence, perhaps a quarter of a mile away, gave onto a road. They headed for it with renewed energy.

In Detroit, Dinkuhl got in touch with Awkright of Genetics Div. Over Dinkuhl's shoulder, Charles saw the interior of the office to which he had been taken by Dinkuhl as the first step in his private commitment. Awkright's broad freckled face came into focus as Dinkuhl adjusted the controls.

Awkright said: "Hiram! So they let you loose?"

"Call me Houdini," Dinkuhl said. "Can you pick us up—Fourth and Eisenhower? We don't want to stay on public view any longer than we have to."

"Be right around." Awkright grinned. "Someone's been looking for you. For Charlie, anyway."

Awkright appeared in a few minutes in Dinkuhl's ramshackle auto; the smell of petrol went ahead of it as well as behind. Dinkuhl and Charles climbed in.

Charles said: "A good way of traveling incognito, this."

Awkright laughed. "I borrowed this while you were away, Hiram. Hope you didn't mind. You mean someone's still after you? I thought you were with UC."

"That was Telecom we just got away from," Dinkuhl remarked. "Where are you heading—not my place? They're likely to be dropping in again with false beards and astarate phials."

"My place," Awkright said. "I told you—Charlie already has a visitor."

Charles said: "Look, you mean there's someone out there waiting to see me? Anything but that."

The auto drew up before a big apartment block fronting the lake. The three of them went inside and took a lift to the top floor. Awkright whistled sharply at the door. He grinned at Charles.

"I warned the visitor we were coming."

The door opened and they went through into the lobby. Awkright said: "You go ahead, Charlie. Straight through to the lounge. I want to show Hiram something."

There was no doubt that something was waiting for him. He pushed the door open and walked into the lounge—a big bright airy room with a lake view. Someone was standing by the main window, looking out over the waters. She turned as she heard him come in. It was Sara.

Charles went right over to her. She smiled, hesitantly and then with warmth. He took her by the elbows, eager to feel the realness, the solidity, of her body. He wanted to bring her closer, to turn the knowledge of her return to him into the conviction of embrace. He was fairly sure she would not refuse him this time, either. But something prevented him. Instead he took one of her hands between his own, caressing it.

"Sara," he said. "How did you get away? Who was it took you?"

She said: "Get away? There wasn't any difficulty. Why should there be?"

"But you were captured in the first place—by someone? It was made to look like suicide."

"Captured, but very politely." She shivered. "That was the unpleasant part. A pre-set lock was put on the gyro controls. After about five minutes I found the controls just didn't respond. I had to sit there while the gyro took me."

"Took you? Where?"

"Sacramento. In the first place."

"Sacramento. Atomics!"

"Of course. I was taken into the Atomics HQ building. They were very nice about everything, and most apologetic. They had had to pick me up, they said, for questioning on a matter of what they called managerial importance. I was to have a bed there for the night, and leave for Philadelphia the next morning."

"You couldn't get any messages out, of course?"

"Well, no. I was fed up about that. But it was understandable. They gave me a direct undertaking that I would be a free agent again in three days, and I had to be content with it." Her face clouded. "During that time, Daddy—you know. But even that wasn't their fault. They asked me whether my disappearing for three days would be likely to have any serious effect on him; they were willing to pick him up as they had done me, if I preferred it. It was my error of judgment. I didn't want him to have the shock of being captured; I guess I underestimated the shock to him of having that happen to me."

"What happened—when you got to Philadelphia?"

"I saw Raven."

Charles whistled. Raven was Chief Director of Atomics, Chairman of the Council of Managerials.

"And . . . ?"

"I liked him. In fact I think he's the first person I've met over here that I've genuinely respected."

Charles said: "He sounds a regular guy. Not the kind who would be trying to get you to complete Dai's work for the benefit of his own managerial at all."

Sara released her hand. "Come and sit down." She led the way over to a wallseat.

"He did want something, though. Can you tell me what it was he wanted?"

Sara fixed her eyes on him. "He wanted me to transfer from UC to Atomics. Officially, and above board. I can tell you that he would like you to do the same."

Charles stared back at her—in amazement. He said:

"You don't mean—you consented? That you applied for transfer?"

From a pocket she took the Atomics flame badge, and pinned it on her tunic. "Yes. I didn't wear this at the beginning because I wanted to explain things to you." Her face softened. "Charles, I should have liked to talk it over with you first, but then they had to tell me that you had been captured by Telecom. They were trying to get you released, but meanwhile what was there to do?"

"Go back to UC. Why not?"

"UC," Sara said, "is so ineffective as to be impossible. The only Managers they've got that are any good are those who, like Ledbetter, are careerists. When Dai disappeared, the Atomics Contact Section were onto it. They tried to get co-operation from UC—from the top, from Graz—but they didn't even know what had been happening in their own laboratories, and didn't care either."

"They didn't know," Charles said, "because Ledbetter had been routing the important stuff through to Telecom."

"That's what I mean," she said. "Ineffective. They still didn't act when I disappeared, or even when Ledbetter

91

had you picked up. And meanwhile they had allowed the lab to be raided and anything that was of any value picked up."

Charles remembered Humayun's reports arriving at The Cottage; of course, Telecom would have got them.

"Yes," he said. "I know about that."

"You see," she said. She showed him her wrist, and the small radio banded to it. "With this, I can call help from Atomics at any time. If I had gone back to UC it would merely have been a matter of presenting myself as a sitting duck to whichever managerial felt like taking aim."

Reluctantly, he began to see her point of view. He himself had been shocked enough by having the familiar world split and quake beneath his feet, and he had not been an exile, in a strange land, a strange world almost.

"It wasn't as though I had any ties to UC, was it? They took us in when we came over from Siraq, but any managerial would have done. We were skilled technicians—Dai and myself, that is. They didn't do anything for Daddy."

"I suppose not. And you're working for them?"

She said frankly: "Not very well. I suppose I'm the collaborative type—I don't work terribly well on my own."

"But how does it happen that you're here—in Awkright's suite? He's not working for Atomics, too?"

"I was flown over here. Three or four hours ago, Telecom alerted their whole organization for triple security checking. Atomics guessed what it meant—that you and Dinkuhl had got clear somehow. The Telecom line seemed to be directed toward Canada, but the Atomic guess was that you would be heading this way. They knew something of Dinkuhl's circle—more than Dinkuhl would like to think, I fancy—and assumed he would get in touch with Awkright as soon as possible. As he did, of course." Her hand moved, to touch his own. "You didn't mind my coming over to meet you?"

He smiled, grasping her fingers. "No."

"Not even when I come as an emissary of a strange managerial, trying to seduce you from your duty?"

"It's always nice to have someone try to seduce you, even when you have no intention of giving way." He grinned. "Isn't it?"

She looked at him appraisingly for a moment, and then colored. "I suppose so."

He thought for a moment. "You do recognize that my duty should be towards UC—my own managerial?"

She shook her head definitely. "No. I was looking at it from the point of view I was afraid you might adopt. But I'm not going to argue about that. Will you come over and see Raven? I can promise you that you can do what you like afterward. There will be no question of holding you against your will."

He said: "Of course I'll come. It will be quite an experience seeing Raven, in any case."

With relief, she said: "I'm glad."

He warned her: "That doesn't mean I'm transferring."

She shrugged, very prettily. "As long as you're coming."

Something that had been teasing Charles' mind returned to bother him now.

He said: "Your watch . . ."

She lifted her finger, looking at him curiously. It was the same watch, or a duplicate.

"You got it back, then," he said.

"Got it back? Oh, I see what you mean. I didn't know you knew about that. I put it in to Allied Electrical for recharging during that week end. Daddy said he would pick it up for me on the Sunday afternoon—he had to go fairly near the automat delivery—but he forgot. His memory was not very good the last few years. He was going to have it sent on to me, but of course . . . I had it sent on to Philadelphia eventually."

Charles said: "Well, I'm damned! As simple an explanation as that. It was that watch that convinced me you really were alive."

She smiled. "Well, I am."

"Yes, but the evidence was unsound."

"Does the evidence matter?"

The grave air of formality, to some extent characteristic of all Atomics posts, was paramount at the Philadelphia HQ. The Chief Director's private office was a long room, with one window on the courtyard and the other on Philadelphia, spread out thirty floors beneath. The desk the Chief Director was using was the one by the courtyard window. The uniformed, precise flunkies ushered Charles and Sara in, and Raven stood up.

"I had the pleasure of seeing you approach, from my window. Miss Koupal, I am very glad you were successful in your mission. And you, too, Mr. Grayner—it was very good of you to be willing to put some of your time at my disposal."

Atomics for some reason retained the archaic forms of address in polite conversation.

Charles said: "Naturally, Chief Director, it's an honor to be invited to meet you."

Raven directed his attention to Sara. "Do take a seat, Miss Koupal. And you, Mr. Grayner."

Sara remained standing. She said: "I think it would be better, sir, if I left the room for the present." She glanced sideways at Charles. "Mr. Grayner knows of my transfer, and knows something of my views on it. I don't think it would help at all for me to stay."

"As you feel best," Raven said. He nodded to the two flunkies by the door, and they opened it again to let Sara out. "You will be within call?"

She nodded. "In the garden." She smiled at Charles, and left.

Raven said: "I think an entirely private conversation would be most satisfactory, don't you, Mr. Grayner? Rogers, Barczywski—wait outside, please."

The doors closed, and they were alone in the long and carefully ordered room. It had been built, and furnished, a long time ago; this was one of the first major edifices of the managerial world.

"You will have a chair, anyway, Mr. Grayner," Raven said. "Cigar, cigarette?"

Charles took the chair indicated, and a cigarette from the box. "Thank you, Chief Director."

Raven went through the motions preparatory to lighting a cigar. He chuckled; it was a restrained but friendly expression.

"If you were to decide to come over to us—I say *if*, Mr. Grayner—it would be incumbent on you to address me as 'sir.' We have our little ways which must be preserved, *ruat coeli*. Am I right in taking it that you would not find an insuperable objection in that small point?"

The flame moved over to him, and he lit up. He smiled. "No. No objection, sir."

"Well," Raven said easily. "That's something. I always prefer to start off with a measure of agreement, however tiny it may be."

He paused, drawing on his cigar, and Charles waited. While he waited, he studied the man.

He was a little under average height, and slimly built. He wore London clothes—a dark rust suit with a lime shirt and cravat—and wore, as a button-hole ornament, a white carnation. His features were somewhat sharp in outline but entirely relaxed in expression; it was impossible to imagine him getting excited over anything. He was probably in his early sixties; his hair had already turned white, and to good effect.

Raven said: "Now, we can get to the business. I want to put things in their perspective. You are, I am sure, a shrewd and eminently sensible young man, but with the experiences you have so recently had, it would be surprising if your judgment had not been knocked a little out of true. And then, for some time now you have had the advantage of the company of Mr. Dinkuhl, a man of acute and perspicacious intelligence but of rather fixed ideas." He glanced at Charles. "Could you, I wonder, give me some idea of your present views?"

"On what?"

"On fundamentals. On society."

"It's rather hard to explain," Charles said. Raven looked at him benevolently, encouragingly. "Until the recent events you mentioned, I took things for granted. I think that what has probably surprised and shocked me more than anything else has been the realization of the mistrust and hostility that exists between managerials. The world seems to have broken up, and it isn't easy to put the pieces together again. Dinkuhl's group of malcontents —you seem to know about them—and the Cometeers— and you probably know about them, too—and then finding that Telecom had access to all my records— through Ledbetter, I suppose. Now you have my records as well. The whole set-up seems to be riddled with double-crossing."

Raven nodded. "Not a very pretty picture, is it? The spectacle of a society chasing its tail, right hand fighting left hand, for the possession of the skills of three people —two of whom are not even its own children—is one to strike fear. I suppose Mr. Dinkuhl would describe such a situation as the ultimate throes of decadence."

Charles smiled slightly. "He does."

"And I," said Raven, "must take a large measure of the blame, I suppose. I have been Chief Director of this managerial for fifteen years, and Chairman of the Council for twelve." He leaned forward slightly. "Ten years ago, to the month, I reminded the Council of the urgency of reorganizing the research and technical development sides of managerial life. It was not a new proposition—several of my predecessors had drawn attention to the same need. The matter was ventilated— and dropped. Nothing got done. Shall I tell you what I did? I launched in this managerial a propaganda drive in favor of science and technology. It was directed principally at the class which was then in process of graduating. A bare handful of one hundred twenty-plus IQ candidates volunteered—and every single one proved to have disabling personality characteristics!"

"In UC," Charles said, "there was no question of opting."

Raven smiled. "Nor, in any other year, was there in this managerial. I thought of enforcing the reversal of policy, and even made tentative plans, but it did not prove possible to carry the idea through. There are limits even to the powers of a Chief Director."

Charles said: "Then Dinkuhl was right. This society is too far gone to save itself."

"Sometimes," Raven said, "I have thought that. But, you know, there never has been a historical situation which was final. In any historical situation, the best one can do is to assess probabilities—and after you have assessed probabilities you have still got to decide about taking sides.

"It is here that Mr. Dinkuhl and I part company. Mr. Dinkuhl wants the world to crash. No doubt he has his reasons, but I do not appreciate them, nor share his views. If society is sick and looks like dying, my instinct is to do what little it may be possible for me to do, to save it. The death of any society is a terrible thing, as Mr. Dinkuhl—as a student of history—must know. It may be that people today are not as happy as the TV screens portray them as being. They cannot be, if so many of them have resort to these peculiar rites of damnation associated with the comet that happens to be visiting us. But I regard the kind of unhappiness they may now have as different in kind from the utter misery and wretchedness that would attend a breakdown in civilized life. It may be a long pull—it may be an entirely vain pull—to get society back on its feet, but I see no harm in trying it."

Ceasing to speak, Raven kept an inquiring look directed on Charles' face. It was impossible not to be impressed by the man's realism and confidence; nor to fail to compare it favorably with Dinkuhl's realism and despair.

"This is the picture I give you, Mr. Grayner. Either you help to destroy managerialism, or help to save it by working on the diamond-solar power source for Atomics. You will be saving, as I have explained, something very imperfect, but destruction is a terrible thing. Should you choose what seems to me the more human course, then you must decide in what direction your help will be of the greatest value. Were other things equal, I should counsel you to work on behalf of your own managerial, for a number of reasons which I will not go into now. But I don't think other things are equal, and I do not think you yourself think so. I ask you to throw in your lot with us, because it is my own belief that we are most capable of helping you and of using your work wisely." He paused. "You might like time to think matters over?"

Charles said: "You already have Sara. If I should ask for transfer as well—aren't UC going to object to this wholesale suborning of their research workers?"

Raven nodded. "It is very likely. But one of the few intermanagerial regulations the Council did agree on was that entailing the full and free right of transfer, with the consent of the person seeking transfer and the new managerial. The consent of the original managerial is specifically not required." He smiled. "Although it was much before my time, I believe I am right in saying that United Chemicals, along with Steel, Allied Electrical and a few others, formed the group that urged the regulation, and that this managerial opposed it in the first place—it was used in a campaign against us. Things make the round. Anyway, you may leave UC's objections to me. It's my job to deal with them."

"One question, sir. You haven't got Humayun?"

"No."

"And you don't know where he is?"

"We have had some lines to work on. Frankly, we know very little yet. He may even be genuinely dead."

"You know that he is the real brain behind the diamond power source—that the original work was all his?"

"We know that. Let me ask you a question, Mr.

Grayner. What stage would you say the work has reached?"

"Development stage. When I first examined it, I wanted to pass it on for routine development—the essential creative work had been completed. Sara persuaded me to carry on for a time. Of course, I did not know then that there was no one in fact capable of doing the development work."

"And how long, in your view, should the development work take?"

Charles shrugged. "It's practically impossible to give an answer—snags always crop up, but you can't estimate the size of the snags nor their number in advance. Not less than three months, I should say. And probably not more than a year." He glanced at Raven. "Once again, it's worth remembering that even if you hold two out of three, it's the third that's the heavyweight."

"I'm not so sure. Humayun may or may not be able to work faster than you and Sara, whoever he is working for. I doubt if he will be able to work much faster?"

"Probably not. The snags stage tends to level things out."

"And our chief concern is to prevent whoever is using Humayun from having the monopoly on the completed invention. For that purpose any fairly close finish will do."

Charles said: "Yes. I see that." He looked around, at the dignified solidity of his surroundings. Suddenly he didn't want to leave them. Raven would let him go if he wanted to—but where should he go? And how would he remain free from Ledbetter and the others? And was he prepared to lose Sara, so recently found again?

He said: "I'll transfer. I'll work for you, sir."

Charles found it difficult to make up his mind about Sara. It had been inevitable, as he saw, that the course of his acquaintance with her—knowing her for so short a time and then separated suddenly and left to brood about her under very abnormal circumstances—should have produced an uncertainty when he found her again; but the uncertainty seemed to be more than was natural. He found a softness in her which was disconcertingly unfamiliar.

The explanation dawned on him unexpectedly. He had left out half of the equation; accounting for the effect of shock on his own attitude he had not remembered that Sara's shock had been a worse one. It would naturally produce changes in her.

Having come to this view, he was prepared to make excuses. She had already, it appeared, been two or three days in the lab, but nothing substantial was there to show for it. He suggested that she should sketch out again her scheme for the rectifier, and she retired into her small office—they had one each—to get on with this. He himself was checking the installation of the scaifes, when the wall screen glowed with a call from the roof lobby. Charles smiled. It was Dinkuhl.

Dinkuhl said: "Charlie boy, so they tied you down already. Any chance of your taking a break for coffee?"

"I have it on the job. Should be up soon. Why not come down and have it here?"

Dinkuhl looked around him with interest when he was brought in. He shook his head, wonderingly.

"Not that I know anything about anything, but how does this stack up against the set-up Ledbetter arranged? As good?"

"A good deal better. We operate smoothly in Atomics —smoothly and fast."

Dinkuhl grinned. "Ah, the new-fledged patriot! You moved fast, all right. I always had my doubts about making a pessimist of you. There was one argument you kept at the back of your mind. Where is the argument, by the way?"

"The argument?"

"Sara. I've been painting a sign for you. 'Here is good horse to hire. Here you may see Charlie the married man.'"

"Not quite as bad as that yet. Or as good. Here she is."

Sara came out of her office. She had the sketch in her hand. She stopped when she saw Dinkuhl.

Charles said: "This is Hiram, Sara."

Dinkuhl said: "I've seen your picture, lady. But you look nicer."

She smiled. "Thank you. Charles has told me about you."

"About our death-defying escape from an impregnable fortress?"

Sara laughed. "I'm glad to know you, Hiram."

Dinkuhl looked at her searchingly. "You are?"

Charles said: "You've got that sketch? Run it through the projector, will you?"

Dinkuhl looked at the screen with interest. "Doesn't mean a damn thing. Is that the super-diamond-bomb or a section of the New York subway?"

"Neither." Charles flicked a circle round a salient point on the pilot screen and its blown-up counterpart glowed on the wall screen. "Only a rectifier. But a rather unusual one, and most elegant. Sara's work."

Dinkuhl said: "Tell your Uncle Hiram how it works, honey."

Sara gestured toward Charles. "Charles makes the explanations. I'm just the help."

"Wouldn't help to tell you, Hiram," Charles said. "No chance of your ignorance becoming vincible."

"I guess not." Dinkuhl turned to Sara again. "You both look happy. What's it like being in Atomics? You got the secret of ultimate bliss? Think I should maybe join up, too?"

"Why not?"

"Yes, why not?" Dinkuhl echoed. "It makes a nice bolt-hole. Comes the big bang, bolt-holes are going to be handy. They give you at least five minutes extra, before someone comes along and pumps gas in from the top."

Grinning, Charles switched the screen off.

"You're an anarchist, Hiram, and anarchists always underestimate the reorganizational powers of society."

"Five minutes," Dinkuhl insisted. "Five minutes, and then a gentle hissing sound." He shot a glance at Sara. "What do you think, honey?"

She said: "You may be right, I suppose. But we might as well try to do what we can while we have the chance."

"Pollyanna in her moated grange," Dinkuhl remarked, "believing where she cannot prove."

Sara smiled. "I suppose so."

Charles said: "Philosophy—even so wise and bitter a philosophy as yours, Hiram—must attend on more practical matters. Sara, I'd like you to tell me what you think of installing the polishing bench in the little room. You coming along, Hiram? Do you know anything about diamond polishing benches?"

"As much as I do about rectifiers. I'll stick here and steal the odd secret to flog to Ledbetter. Maybe there's a chance I can put KF back in the black."

When they returned to the main room, perhaps five minutes later, Dinkuhl was sitting on one of the stools watching the TV screen. He switched off as they came in.

"In the act," Charles said. "Cosy Bright?"

"The practised ascetic knows where to draw a line. Red League's good enough for me. Whenever the springs of optimism begin to well up in my unlikely breast, I only have to watch the old Red League for a couple of minutes. Realism infallibly sets in again."

"Preserve your perspective," Charles said. "At least, Red League's no worse than it would have been in the later Roman Empire, if they had had TV then."

Dinkuhl shook his head. "Inferior by omission. We haven't got any Christians, and all the lions have been emasculated. I won't keep you two from the great work any longer. Nice to see the place, though. I'll drop in again."

"You were going to have coffee with us. It'll be up any minute now."

"Drink a toast," Dinkuhl said, "to absent friends. I've remembered there's someone I want to look up while I'm here, and I've got to be back in Detroit for the

102

afternoon." He bowed solemnly to Sara. "I am glad to have known you, too, lady. I hope I shall see more of you in the future."

"We'll always be glad to see you here, Hiram. Both of us."

Dinkuhl nodded. "I'm touched."

Sara and Charles worked late that night and started early the next morning. The first hitch occurred soon after lunch; the plasbestos they were using for heat insulation turned out to be badly flawed. Charles got through to Conway, who was handling the supplies for them. He was a man of melancholy appearance, but of surprising charm and forcefulness whenever the need arose. He listened to Charles' explanation carefully.

He said: "UC material. Not really surprising. But we asked for grade A plus and we paid grade A plus prices for it. Leave it to me. I'll send a man down right away to collect a sample of the dud stuff."

"And replacement?" Charles asked. "How long will that take?"

Conway smiled. "UC replacement schedules are twenty-four-hour jobs. Normally they take two to three days. I'll have the stuff with you in six hours."

As the glow died from the screen, Sara said:

"Six hours. We could take a break."

Charles nodded. There were a number of minor jobs which they could get on with, but he didn't have much enthusiasm for them.

"What do you suggest?"

"It's a long time since I went airsphering. There's a good wind. It ought to be fun."

The airsphere hangar was reached through the roof-garden. Above and beyond the summer through which they walked, the sky was gray and angry, and tossed with scudding clouds. Airsphering afficionados had always held, with near fanatical dogmatism, that the sport should not be described as airsphering at all with winds at less than force 5, but, as in most sports, they were outnumbered by the casuals. The hangar was full. Atomics HQ apparently did not boast many really keen airspherers.

"Singles?" Charles asked.

The singles were the small one-man spheres; there were also doubles, and multiples capable of taking parties of six.

"I'd rather a double."

Her look was of uncertainty and trust; very feminine and very flattering.

He said: "My preference, too. All right if we take a blue?"

The blues were spheres whose plaspex was delicately tinged with azure, and whose Sokije valves had hair-trigger sensitivity. It made them fast in response, but correspondingly risky in inexpert hands. Charles had not done a great deal of airsphering, but he knew himself to be competent at it. Just at present, he recognized with inner amusement, he was playing up to the situation caused by Sara's choice of a double: the masterful male.

They pulled the sphere clear of the hangar, and climbed in. There were two seats, each with controls but the controls had automatic cut-offs which prevented both being used together. The seats were adjustable from ninety degrees to a hundred and eighty. Charles took the right-hand seat and controls. He decompressed and there was the slight hiss of air being driven out and helium taking its place. The sphere rose gently through the quiet air trapped in the roof-garden. Then it emerged, above the conditioning range, above the plane of sunlets, and the wind struck it like a giant's bat, lifting and swinging it away into the outfield. The blustering sky was suddenly all round them; the shock of the transition was a thrill in itself.

"Cut off," Sara said. "Quite cut off from everything."

They had jumped to a thousand feet in a few seconds, and were still rising. The Atomics building had fallen away behind them; with the plaspex giving them vision all round—above and below and to all the corners of the horizon—they could see with sharp clarity just how isolated they were.

Philadelphia was drifting away, too. There were a few gyros battling through the wind and a stratoliner was coming in to land at the field by the city's northern limits. They were in a private world, more isolated with each passing moment.

"See the sun?" Charles asked. "The real sun?"

"Love to."

They were in cloud, a sea of mist pressing about them, now lighter, now darker. Like a bubble bursting through depths of water, the sphere burst free. The sunlight was radiant everywhere, and reflected from the dazzling white surface of the world through which they had just emerged. That world was one of continual movement —a plain where crevasses sprang out and were swallowed up again, where tentacles, reaching slimly from the ground, became squat towers until the towers themselves collapsed back into the ground from which they had risen. And all white, all feathery snow.

Sara gasped. "It's wonderful."

"Perhaps we should stay here."

She smiled. "And live on?" She poked in the side locker and produced three bars of candy. "On these?"

"On angel's food," Charles said. "On light."

The air was less turbulent here; the sphere continued to rise, but only slowly. The enchanted landscape merged more and more into a great glistening plain stretching in every direction. Charles compressed slightly, and the sphere began to drop. The landscape opened up again, in shifting whorl and contour. They grazed the woolly surface and he maneuvered the controls with fine delicacy so that they bounced along, as though sledding on living snow. At times a dazzling upflung cliff would appear in front of them, and the sphere would plough through its pearl-gray interior, to re-emerge into sunshine. And again the cloud beneath them would open up into some vast ravine, through which, once or twice, there were

105

brief glimpses of the other world two thousand feet below—the world that held them on an elastic rope, the managerial world.

Sara said: "Up. Charles, up now."

"To the sun?"

"Or higher."

As he decompressed to the full, the sphere shot up, and cliffs and ravines dwindled again and were lost in the all-extending, all-embracing white of the plain. Soon it was bereft of all individual features. It was a carpet of dazzling snow that stretched in every direction to the downward curving horizon. It was difficult to believe in the real existence of the world beneath the cloud belt.

Charles adjusted the controls for height stabilization. The altimeter needle bobbed gently just above the 3,000 figure. He did not know what horizontal orientation they might have; the airspheres were equipped with position-fixing equipment based on the triangulation of Telecom's beacon transmitters, but there was no hurry to find out how far they might have drifted from Philadelphia. However far it might be, it was always possible to find a return current at some altitude. It was enough at present to relax in a warm sea of golden light, under an azure sky.

Sara slipped her tunic-coat off. Beneath it she was wearing a short one-piece dress; it was a shade of blue that went well with her dark coloring. She pushed her chair back to horizontal, and lay back. She looked up at Charles, shading her eyes against the sunlight.

"Aren't you hot?"

He slipped his own coat off, and tossed it to the back of the airsphere; it lay beside Sara's discarded garment. There was a significance about that, which he was not sure if he wanted to think about. He was wearing the sleeveless shirt and shorts he normally wore when off duty in conditioned atmospheres. The sun was very pleasantly warm on his arms and legs.

He looked down at Sara. Her eyes half closed, she was looking at him quizzically. She showed to her best advantage: the bronze of her skin against the deep crimson of the airfoam, and the faintly blued white of the far-away background.

He said: "I think I might relax, too."

She smiled, but made no reply. He pushed his own chair back, and turned to face her. The smile still lingered.

"I wondered . . ."

Her lips barely parted. "Yes?"

"A scientific question."

"If I can help you . . ."

"The well-known Siraqi inhibitions—I wondered if they functioned with the same precision at all altitudes."

The smile deepened. "I should think, a very interesting question. What would be the scientific approach to it?"

"Experimental."

He moved toward her. Her willingness was certain even before she opened her arms to him.

Dinkuhl had explained that he was only stopping off at Philadelphia in the course of a trip to New York. He had had the idea of making the detour simply in order to have a meal with Charles, on the way. On his expense account, he further explained. He was at Oak Ridge, which was the Atomics men-only club, so Charles had to make his excuses and leave Sara.

Dinkuhl had tall glasses of hot rum and ginger waiting when Charles arrived.

He said: "Drink it up, Charlie boy. How's life. You look like a cat that's been living on alcoholic cream."

Charles eased himself into a chair, and took the glass from the adjoining table. "Very fair. No complaints. How about you? No trouble from Ledbetter?"

It had been Charles' idea that Dinkuhl should be given an Atomics bodyguard in view of his having been concerned with Charles both in imprisonment and escape. Atomics had been willing, but Dinkuhl had laughed at the idea. In his view, Telecom would be anxious to keep the defeat of their plans as private as possible. Taking it out on him would merely be an exercise in vindictiveness; it would give them no material advantage and might well provoke the reverse, should Charles urge Atomics into retaliatory action.

"Trouble?" Dinkuhl laughed. "You know, the first morning back, Gillray called me up. Asked me if I'd been taking a holiday. If that character were any smoother, his face would slide off the screen."

They had lunch. While they talked, Charles was aware that there was something worrying Dinkuhl; he talked and joked but the talk and the jokes were perfunctory. He made no attempt to find out what it was; Dinkuhl was not the kind of person who encouraged solicitous probing into his troubles. But Dinkuhl brought things out into the open himself, over coffee.

"I've got a problem, Charlie boy," he said.

Charles nodded. "Unusual. So unusual that I'll offer my help. If I can help."

"I'd appreciate your advice. It's not personal. That is, it's not my worry actually. It's Burt's."

"Awkright's?"

"Yes. You know your new outfit used him to get in touch with us—with Sara. They spun him a yarn about the wonders of Atomics Contact Section that enabled them to know he was one of my little gang of rebels— by God, if the PRO's don't get the fattest salary in the Contact Sections they ought to, the line of guff they hand out. He was happy enough thinking it was just Atomics that were exceptionally clever—still is. I wasn't as happy as he was. I started looking around. I found that Atomics were not the only people in the know— very far from it. I had known that Telecom knew, of course—they had to know to pick you up through me. But it was more than two, even—Mining, Steel . . . Genetics Division—"

"Genetics?"

"Yes. Burt's own managerial. The boys took some precautions, but not that many. We thought we weren't

108

interesting. We weren't, but I guess it kept the Contact brigades in practice. We are all neatly docketed and ticketed."

"For action?"

"For information. The boys are all useful workers, and they find that useful workers mostly have aberrations nowadays; they put up with them providing there's nothing dangerous there."

Charles said absently: "Then I don't see what's worrying you."

"Burt," Dinkuhl said, "is a more complex person than you might guess. I've known him for some time, and I know what he would do if he found out his seditious associations with me and the boys were known to the Genetics brass. He'd transfer—anywhere so long as it was outside Genetics and away from Detroit. He can't stand to be pitied or laughed at."

"Most folk don't enjoy it."

"They get by; Burt wouldn't. You get it, though? Do I tell him the truth or not? He's not likely to find out unless I do tell him. If I tell him, he'll leave and he'll be unhappy. If I don't tell him . . . where I want your advice is there: a guy's living in a fool's paradise—which is best, to leave him lie or to give him the jolt?"

Charles' thoughts were partly on Sara, partly on the problem of the miniaturization of a thermoelectric conversion system. He gave Dinkuhl's question lukewarm attention, until he realized it was a question of principle on which advice was being sought. He brought his mind to focus.

"I should tell him. People are always entitled to be told the truth. No one has the right to decide in advance that it's bad for someone else to know the truth about his own affairs. Whatever it is, and whatever he may do as a result."

Dinkuhl pursed his lips. "I guess you're right. Maybe I was thinking of myself; I'll be sorry as hell if Burt does light out for somewhere else."

"Tell you what," Charles said. "Affiliate KF to Atomics

109

and bring the works over to Philly. Raven would fork out, if only to make Telecom sore."

Dinkuhl smiled. "I'll think of that. I'll let you know—I'll be dropping in on you again soon."

Things ran smoothly meanwhile. Raven himself dropped in at the laboratory now and then; he showed a good deal of friendliness and an intelligent interest. Charles found him standing beside him one day while he was completing the polishing of a stone. He heard Raven's voice above the nervous grinding whine of the scaife.

"Mr. Grayner, are you finding it pleasant working here?"

"Very pleasant, sir."

Raven looked about with an air of deprecation. "Not magnificent. Not at all magnificent. You would have fared better with Telecom; from the material point of view, at least. Still, we must try to do what we can for you. Any complaints, for instance? Are there any complaints, Mr. Grayner?"

Charles hesitated very briefly; the hesitation was involuntary, and he spoke quickly to cover it up.

"No complaints, sir. I have everything I want."

"You and Miss Koupal are getting on all right together?"

He said, with no hesitation this time: "Very well."

"That's good. I hope you won't hesitate to come to me if there should be anything. Don't hesitate to waste my time. It is yours that is more valuable."

Raven went, with his jaunty old man's step, and Charles had to master an impulse to go after him, or to call him back. He mastered it as he had covered up the earlier hesitation, and for the same reason. It was not that he doubted Raven's willingness, nor even his ability, to help him. It was that it was impossible to frame any of his doubts or his worries without criticizing, if only by implication, Sara.

110

Outside the laboratory, their life together proceeded very harmoniously. They did most things and went to most places together. Charles did not let his doubts carry over to spoil this part of their association. All of love was a new experience for him, and he was determined it should not be spoiled in any way.

They spent a lot of time airsphering—mostly together, but occasionally each in a single bubble. Then there would be the delight of chasing each other over the invisible hills and valleys of the air. Along the rivers of the wind they would chase each other, and they were rivers capable of turning, without warning, into precipitous waterfalls that plunged the spheres hundreds of feet, either up or down, in an instant. Close on her heels, Charles might suddenly find himself looking down on her far below, or gazing up, blinded by sun, to where her sphere drifted high and remote.

The Alleghenies provided them with a pleasure ground. There they could ride the updrafts, close against the rocky mountain sides, and glide dangerously alongside the knife edged spurs that could so easily rip the plaspex skin, spilling the sphere's occupant down great cliffs of fall to distant midget valleys.

And, of course, there was the delight of bringing the spheres in to some sun-splashed ledge of rock, on the world's roof, of tethering them to the mountain face with impact suckers, of eating and drinking in that warm silent isolation, of sitting and talking or simply sun-bathing. Of making love.

Charles had sent Sara to check personally some supplies that had been queried by Conway when Dinkuhl paid his next visit.

He said: "Hi, Charlie."

Charles said: "Burt asked for transfer?"

Dinkuhl nodded. "He left last night. That advice you gave me. Tell the truth and let the chips fly what way they will. You still think it's good?"

111

"The best. But I'm sorry you've lost Burt. Where's he gone to?"

"Lignin. Somewhere north of Finland. Lignin should be pleased all right. They're shorter of good men than most managerials. And they're all short, with the notable and glorious exception of Atomics. Sara?"

"Checking supplies. She'll be back soon."

Dinkuhl leaned back against one of the benches; he had a restless look and his voice had taken on the slightly affected drawl that indicated some inner excitement.

"That the set-up now?" he asked. "You do the work and she checks supplies in? I thought her middle name was Einstein."

Charles said angrily: "What the hell do you mean by that, Hiram?"

"Brother," Dinkuhl said softly, "you're worried. You're plenty worried. Tell Uncle Hiram."

Charles stared at him. "For God's sake! Have you gone crazy? Who's worried?"

"What is it, Charlie?" Dinkuhl asked. "She isn't as bright any longer? She doesn't grasp things that should be simple going? You wonder even if maybe she had a knock on the head during that fortnight you were apart?"

Charles restrained his voice to quietness. "I don't know what's got into you. Burt transferring, maybe. Anyway, I want you to keep it for somewhere else, Hiram." He turned away. "You'll be welcome in a different mood."

"I'll carry the invitation in my heart. Here the lady is now. Hi, Sara. Been copying any good sketches lately?"

Charles had no idea what Dinkuhl was talking about, but the tone was unmistakably offensive. He expected Sara to flare up or to treat him with icy contempt. She did neither. She said placatingly:

"Glad you managed to get along, Hiram."

Dinkuhl watched her for a moment. Then he smiled. "What we all need," he remarked, "is a drink. You both have a drink?"

Charles hesitated. Sara said: "Be glad to."

Dinkuhl brought a flask out of his back pocket. It had two small plastobeakers attached. He filled them, and looked about him inquiringly.

"A glass for Uncle Hiram? You find me one, Sara?"

While Sara was getting it, Dinkuhl picked up the two already filled. He gave one to Charles; the other he held in his hand, holding it with his palm cupped above it. When Sara came back, he gave it to her, and took the glass she brought and poured out a tot for himself.

"To all honest men," he said. He bowed to Sara. "And honest women."

She coughed a little as she drank. "What is it?"

"All right? Liqueur grappa. I have a source."

She smiled. "A good one, I should say."

"All my sources are." Dinkuhl considered her speculatively. "You know something? Charles here has been telling me he's disappointed in you. He thinks you're lying down on the job. He—"

Charles stepped across to stand in front of Dinkuhl. He said tightly:

"I don't know what's got into you, Hiram. But, for the last time, lay off. Lay off!"

Dinkuhl said: "You know, I never met Sara. But I know enough about her to know she wouldn't have needed your help in a slanging match, Charlie." To Sara, he said: "Well, honey?"

She said uncertainly: "I feel dizzy."

Dinkuhl took her gently round the shoulders. "Come and lie down, honey. You need rest. Easy now. Couch over here."

He got her on to the couch, and made her comfortable. She shook her head, as though trying to shake off cobwebs.

Dinkuhl said: "You're going to sleep, honey."

His voice was significant, and as though in response she jerked up. "You mean . . . ? The drink!"

Charles demanded: "Just what have you been doing?"

Dinkuhl said gently: "What's your name, honey? Before you go to sleep, what's your name?"

113

Her speech was becoming slurred; unable to sustain the effort she had made, she sank back again. "Sara Koupal. You know—"

Dinkuhl shook his head. "No. Not that. Your real name."

She tried to speak again, but it was beyond her. For a brief moment she looked at them in agony and fear, and then her eyes closed, and she was unconscious. Charles had rushed over to her, and he sat beside her now, holding her limp hand. He turned to look up at Dinkuhl.

"Something good, Hiram. It had better be something good."

Dinkuhl said: "Don't think I'm happy. I wasn't happy when I told Burt, either. That was why I put the question to you the last time I was over. I could see you were happy with the girl, and it made it hard. It was a relief that you should make it so clear things were worrying you, when I came this time. They were, weren't they?"

Charles felt that anger, and every other positive emotion, had been drained from him. He looked at Sara's quietly breathing body. Sara's? A Sara surprisingly unhelpful in the work, a Sara he could almost think of as trying to cover up her own ignorance. The doubts that he had dammed up were now flooding around him; his thoughts bobbed like chips on the tide.

Dinkuhl said: "You see, I had had access to those UC Contact Section reports—they included Sara's psychoplan. A wench of spirit. But even if that line hadn't been so strongly marked, it was still reasonable that a girl who showed herself so clearly to be interested in you should have had a different reaction to me. The first time I came over here, I clowned, I made snide remarks. She took them, like a little woolly lamb. It wasn't right, Charlie. It wasn't right for a normal girl, and it was very wrong for one with a psychoplan like Sara's."

Charles looked at him, and back to the girl's figure.

"You mean, they've done something to her? What? And why, in God's name?"

"That isn't Sara, Charlie. It never was Sara."

Charles shook his head. "I know her. It's Sara. Her voice alone—"

Dunkuhl bent over the girl. He pulled the neck of her tunic down a fraction, and pointed. There was a line on the skin, barely visible, perhaps an inch long.

"Gannery's operation. Re-formation of the vocal cords. You can get precision with it and I guess this job was a precision job."

"How did you know that would be there?"

"It had to be. I knew she was a phony. You remember the time she'd been showing that blueprint-thing on the wall screen? You took her off to show her the diamond polishing bench. I had a look in her little room while you were away. She had been copying that sketch from a photostat of the original that Sara did. Why should she need to copy, unless it was because she wasn't Sara at all? They had primed her well, but you can't prime a person with years of scientific experience."

Charles stared at the motionless girl. "I can't believe it. That little scar . . . it could be something else."

Dinkuhl stood beside him. "You remember being Charlie Macintosh, Charlie? Macintosh was a real guy —works at an obscure GD station in South Africa. Would have been a laugh if you'd met up with him. Burt went to some trouble to pick him: he had to be someone who matched you closely, but with extra flesh at all points. You can build up; you can't whittle down. He had full cheeks, while you have thin ones."

He paused, gazing at the face of the girl who had been Sara. "An interesting face. Good-looking, but not precisely beautiful. The temples bulging a little just above the brow line. Unusual, that."

From his pocket, Dinkuhl took a small knife; he flipped the catch and the sapphire blade leapt out, gleaming dully. Charles watched in fascination as he bent down toward the unconscious face. He heard himself saying: "Stop . . . !" With a deft motion, Dinkuhl sliced the girl's flesh at the base of the forehead.

115

He held up a strip of flesh that he had cut away. There was no bleeding from the incision. The cut had laid bare not flesh but plastic. Now, beyond any doubt, Charles knew he had been loving a mask. Dinkuhl tossed the strip into a disposer; he walked away from the girl, and leaned against a bench on the opposite side of the room. He looked at Charles.

"Well, Charlie boy? What's it going to be?"

Charles said dully: "You tell me. How do you expect I should know?"

"People are always entitled to be told the truth. No, I'm not riding you, Charlie. I'm not the strictly monogamous type, but I can guess how bad it is. This way, though, it's quick. You would have had to find out sooner or later. They still operate on the assumption that scientists are dumb. Hell, you were finding out already. It was better this way."

Charles shook himself. He saw the truth of Dinkuhl's statements, but that still didn't make it easy to act on them. To find that he had been deceived in this way was somehow worse than when he had thought Sara killed. He looked up at Dinkuhl, almost in inquiry.

"Raven?"

"Just a fine old Southern gentleman. Ledbetter was no more than peanuts. Raven's good. All these tricky arrangements made on the assumption that they were going to get you away from Telecom. We only made it easier for him by arranging the break ourselves. Raven's the kingpin, all right. You've reached the managerial top, Charlie. You can't go higher. This is where they put gloves on before they reach for their knives."

Charles looked at Dinkuhl helplessly. "What's the best thing to do? I should like to see Raven. Is that silly?"

"No. Not at all silly. Inevitable, I should say." He glanced around the lab. "I should hazard a guess that the usual precautions are in operation. Even if they aren't, I can think of easier things than just walking out of a place like this. The air of casualness has, to my mind, a somewhat studied look."

116

"I guess so. That kind of crook doesn't take chances."

"Don't be bitter, Charlie—not about individuals. It doesn't pay any percentage." Dinkuhl raised his head slightly. There was the sound of a door sliding open in the lobby. "A visitor. Red-handed. In this same country, and besides, the wench is not dead."

It was Raven himself. He stopped just inside the door. His bright amused eyes took in the tableau—Dinkuhl leaning against the bench, Charles still sitting on the couch beside the girl's recumbent body.

Raven said: "Good morning, Mr. Grayner. And Mr. Dinkuhl." He peered toward the girl. "The lady would appear to be indisposed."

Automatically, Charles said: "Good morning, sir."

Dinkuhl leaned back a little further. He drawled:

"I guess the lady drank something that disagreed with her. Would there be any objection to your introducing her to us, Director, so we shall know whom to apologize to?"

Dinkuhl watched with bland unconcern as Raven walked across to the couch, and bent down to examine the girl. Raven straightened up again a moment later, and looked at them both.

"Would you gentleman object if I were to arrange for Miss Levine to be taken away and put properly to bed? I doubt if she is likely to recover her faculties for some hours yet."

Charles did not say anything. Dinkuhl nodded.

"Go right ahead. It's your home territory. We should appreciate it to have Miss Levine attended to."

Raven went across to the callscreen. They heard him asking for two stretcher-men. Then he switched off and turned his attention back to them. He said:

"This has been rather unfortunate. I had hoped it would be delayed for some time—a few more weeks, at any rate. But we must put up with events as they fall out."

"Life," Dinkuhl said gravely, "is like that. I hope you

will arrange to convey our regrets to Miss Levine when she wakes up. She will understand it was nothing personal."

Raven said: "And you, Mr. Grayner? Your regrets as well?"

The implication was obvious, and Charles resented it. But he was prevented from saying anything immediately by the arrival of the stretcher-men. They put the girl gently on to the stretcher. Raven said: "To her rooms, please, and then get a nurse for her."

Charles felt Raven watching him while the little procession left the room. He said, as the door slid closed behind them:

"A lot of regrets, Director. But they are all concerned with being made a fool of. No regrets about finding the truth out. Assistant Levine was doing her duty, I guess. No one's fault if it came out this way."

"If we must use these titles," Raven said softly, "we should use the right ones. Manager Levine. An exceptionally brilliant and talented young lady, and we are very proud of her."

"With the views I now hold of Atomics," Charles said bitterly, "that fails to surprise me."

"Your views are understandable. They would be understandable even if you had not had the benefit of Mr. Dinkuhl's tutelage. But I hope they will not be permanent. You are an intelligent man, Mr. Grayner—that is not flattery, but a statement germane to the situation. Mr. Dinkuhl is also of high intelligence, but his intellect is hampered by his emotions; particularly by that overriding urge to destruction, which is so marked a feature of his attitude toward society. I have discussed this point with you before."

Dinkuhl said lazily: "That's me. Samson, with each arm around a pillar."

Charles said: "You convinced me that Hiram had taken an unreasonably pessimistic view. But part of the conviction at least was from believing that you, and Atomics, represented something higher than the others."

118

"To my great regret," Raven said, "I felt obliged to give you that somewhat exaggerated impression of my personal integrity. It was made necessary by the experiences you had already undergone. I should like you to believe that I would have preferred to be frank with you or, since I could not be frank, dishonest in the normal human fashion."

"You can tell the truth?"

"From this time on, Mr. Grayner, I shall use nothing else with you. There would be no point."

Charles said: "Where is Sara Koupal? Who has her?"

"I do not know. We have looked very hard and we have not found her—neither her nor Humayun. You can imagine that we have spared no efforts to find both of them. They may be dead. It is a conclusion to which the absence of any information is tending to force us. You see that I am being frank now, Mr. Grayner."

"Are you?" Dinkuhl asked. "Or could you be trying to persuade Charlie that he might as well make do with a near-miss? Another dab of plastic, and Miss Levine's as good as new."

"No, Mr. Dinkuhl," Raven said. "You misjudged me. I was being frank. You are putting things in their worst aspect though I will admit to hoping that Mr. Grayner may overcome his present resentment against Miss Levine. But that was not in my mind at that time." He glanced at Charles. "Miss Levine took this duty on with great reluctance. She accepted the task only on my personal plea, and because she was the one person available who could be made to resemble Miss Koupal physically, and at the same time be capable of deceiving you for a time on points of personality and technical skill. Her failure—for I'm afraid it was failure—in this latter is a pointer to its difficulty. No one else could have done it anywhere near as well."

"She made one big error," Charles commented. "And one easy enough to avoid. Sara is essentially chaste. Didn't her psychoplan show that?"

Raven nodded. "So," he said, "is Miss Levine."

"Then the orders she was given were at fault."

"There was no orders. I think I take your meaning, Mr. Grayner. Whatever may have happened between you was not a part of the attempt to deceive you. You will give me credit, I hope, for not committing so egregious a blunder."

"Then?"

"Mis Levine was surprised—and not pleased, Mr. Grayner—to find her duty in some respects more attractive than she had anticipated. She quickly became fond of you."

"She told you that?"

Raven ran a neatly manicured hand through his white and well-groomed hair.

"She had to, Mr. Grayner. It was necessary, to explain her request to be relieved of her duty."

"She asked that?"

"Three times. The latest occasion was yesterday evening. I was forced to refuse her requests. I told her I hoped that within a week or two you would have settled well enough in this managerial to have the truth explained to you. I did not reckon with Mr. Dinkuhl, who appears to have a talent for unveiling indiscreet secrets."

Incredulously, Charles asked: "You think, under those circumstances, I would have stayed?"

Raven said: "Mr. Dinkuhl, that is a flask I see in your pocket? Might we not all have a drink—unadulterated this time?"

Dinkuhl grinned. He poured into the two plastobeakers and the glass. He retained the beaker the girl had had for himself, and handed the others around.

"I'll take the residual Mickey. Your health, Director."

Raven took the drink, sniffed it, drank, and smacked his lips lightly. "A good liquor, Mr. Dinkuhl."

"I always find the best is good enough."

"A good motto. Now, Mr. Grayner—would you have stayed? I hope you would. I hope you still will."

It was clearly the beginning of a long disquisition. Charles broke in.

"Before you go any further, Director, I should like to express my views on something—on the ties that can exist, that should exist between the man and the managerial. I can see two, and only two: natural loyalty, and trust. I still retained some loyalty to UC after I had seen it as inefficient and corrupt, because the loyalty went back a long way. It isn't possible for me to have that kind of loyalty to Atomics. That's where the necessity for trust comes in. And it's a vulnerable growth. It won't stand up to the kind of treatment you have given it—with whatever good intentions. I can assure you that it is dead. Dead and stinking."

There was a short silence, as though Raven were waiting to be certain that Charlie had finished what he was going to say. Then he said:

"Loyalty to a managerial—trust in a managerial—those are sentiments apt for the lower levels of society. You have left that stage, Mr. Grayner, as Mr. Dinkuhl had done before you. Nor can you get back to it. Could you go back to UC from this managerial? Could you even contemplate such a return? You have joined the emancipated, and perhaps that is your misfortune. But one thing is certain: it doesn't make life easier, and it most certainly does not make the course of your future acts obvious or assured.

"Your disillusion is nothing new to me, Mr. Grayner. I became acquainted with it many years ago. The Chief Director of a managerial is the last person who could possibly be a starry-eyed managerialist. He sees a number of distasteful things, and he is forced to take part in some of them. But he must continue to work through his managerial on behalf of the higher loyalty he holds."

"Which is?" Dinkuhl asked.

"Loyalty to the human race. It is a far-reaching loyalty and not always easy to grasp—it is not *possible* to grasp it until the earlier loyalties have been superseded. But it is, of course, the fundamental loyalty of man."

"And the fundamental loyalty," Dinkuhl suggested,

"demands that Charlie goes on working for Atomics—though you don't need to call it Atomics? What shall we call it? United Preservers of Mankind—how's that?"

Raven was not ruffled. He smiled dismissingly at Dinkuhl.

"Not one of the things I said at our first meeting is invalidated by your discovery that I have been deceiving you in the matter of Sara Koupal. As I have said, it was certain that the deception could not be maintained for very long in any case. I risked the disappointment and resentment that you were bound to feel then because of my confidence in your fundamental level-headedness. And in your ability to rise above your own needs and desires.

"I am asking you to do that now, Mr. Grayner—to forget your personal problems for a moment and to study things in a more general and detached light. The human race is facing one of its moments of decision, and you personally can be of great importance in the way that decision goes. Even without Humayun's discovery, the situation would have been critical, but it now becomes urgently so. I put it to you with all seriousness that the world may be facing devastation."

Dinkuhl said: "Not for the first time. They sacked Cnossos five thousand years ago. And shall Atomics live?"

Raven walked across to Dinkuhl. He stood before him, his hands folded together.

"Have you thought of what the sack of Cnossos must have been like, Mr. Dinkuhl? Is it not possible that the lethargy, the flabbiness of spirit, that you so rightly chide in the world about us may have blinded you to the sleeping furies? For they are no more than sleeping—the Cometeers show us that. It is this social fabric you despise that prevents them from waking. Destroy it, and you will see them rub their eyes."

Dinkuhl looked at him and smiled. "They are rubbing their eyes already, Director. What is more, their bellies are rumbling."

"Do you think, then, that man was made for murder—for torture and rape and brutality?"

For a moment Dinkuhl was silent. He said: "I don't know what he was made for. Maybe he was made to sit in front of a TV screen. If he was, I'll take the torture, rape and brutality; it has a healthy ring to it."

Raven swung around, an easy unhurried movement, to look at Charles.

"This is the point, Mr. Grayner: do you share your friend's view of cataclysms? Do you feel with him that Red League and Cosy Bright cry out for cannibalism as a counterweight? I do not ask you to place any trust in me, nor in this managerial, but I ask you—forgetting your own needs, forgetting Sara Koupal—to answer a question truthfully. The question is this: do you know of any capacity in which you can serve your fellow-men better than—no, as well as!—you can here? Never mind whether they have deserved destruction and damnation. That is the sort of question we can leave to the Cometeers. But from the simple point of view of avoiding pain and suffering, where else can you do as much?"

"One small item," Dinkuhl cut in. "A necessary item on that premise. Charlie produces the power source and the weapon: then he has to trust you for the using of it."

Raven said, with absolute confidence: "I will leave that point to Mr. Grayner. He knows that I have deceived him, but he knows also that I did this with a larger end in view. I apologize for deceiving him, but I do not regret putting the world's needs first. It is precisely because I have already done that, in fact, that I can appeal to him to rely on my integrity in the future."

Dinkuhl said: "Charlie, my view is we've heard enough from Chief Director Raven. We know just what kind of a noble and altruistic lover of mankind he is. I think that at this point we can prepare to move on."

Raven said to Charles: "Well, Mr. Grayner? Destruction or salvage? A corrupt and decadent world—do you destroy it or do you try to mend it?"

Charles stood in silence; he felt that his irresolution must be written all over him. Raven and Dinkuhl were both looking at him—Raven with calm confidence, Dinkuhl with the trace of a mocking grin.

He said: "I don't know—"

Dinkuhl said: "I suppose a key point is whether even now you have all the facts in the situation. All the relevant facts. Has he had all the relevant facts presented, do you think, Director?"

Raven nodded. "As far as I am concerned—yes."

Charles glanced quickly at Dinkuhl; he knew him well enough by now to know that something was due to follow.

"You wouldn't consider it a relevant fact," Dinkuhl asked, "that you have been personally losing ground both on the Atomics Board of Directors and the World Council of Managerials for some years past—that your touching desire to save the world from itself is bound up with an anxiety to restore your own prestige?"

"It would be relevant if it were true. But it is not true."

"The advantage I have over you, Director, is that Charlie has not yet caught me out lying to him. There is a motion down for the next Board meeting of this managerial, expressing no confidence in you as Chief Director and calling for your resignation. It is subscribed by Ramaseshan of New Delhi and Burlitz of Munich." He paused. "You can now remove my advantage by calling your secretary from this room and asking her to put on the screen the draft of agenda for the meeting in question. In case your memory needs refreshing, the meeting will be held on February twenty-third, at New Delhi."

There was a brief silence. On Raven's face there still remained the faint smile he had called up at Dinkuhl's first charge of his personal interest in having Charles in Atomics. He made the gesture Charles had expected him to make on their first meeting; he lifted his hands and examined his nails. The control was admirable.

"I could defend myself, Mr. Dinkuhl," Raven said at last, "but for the second time I have been caught in deception—and this time it was most certainly an error of judgment. Twice is too many."

He shrugged delicately. Dinkuhl was observing him closely.

"So now," Dinkuhl commented, "for our own good, for the good of suffering mankind, and last and least for the good of the prestige of Chief Director Raven, you must—regrettably, regretfully—adopt the methods of such inferiors as Ledbetter. You must use force."

The shrug was repeated, more delicately still. "With very great regret, I assure you, Mr. Dinkuhl. I am not under any illusion that the work will progress as swiftly in such conditions. But there is no alternative."

"Should your colleagues, Ramaseshan and Burlitz, become aware of your having had such a prize and of your having jeopardized it through what they might think of as a desire for personal aggrandizement, I feel your position would become less secure rather than more, Director."

Raven smiled. "I am inclined to agree, Mr. Dinkuhl. Fortunately they are not likely to become aware of it. I have better security control here at Philadelphia than possibly you might imagine."

"I've got a good imagination. I hope you have, too, Director. Just about now, Ramaseshan is receiving a radio report. It explains to him how, for the good of Atomics—we omit mankind for the moment—you took steps to obtain the services of Official Grayner, late of United Chemicals, who is—to your knowledge—the sole person capable of carrying through a project that will bring final power to that managerial which obtains it exclusively. Unfortunately Grayner has been got at by some outside group and either abducted or persuaded to desert. You have reason to think the destination is Asia, and probably India. Ramaseshan's aid in recovering the fugitive will be appreciated. The report is signed Raven."

Raven looked at Dinkuhl. He said slowly: "Your destructive potential is very high, Mr. Dinkuhl."

"Don't bother to make any formal good-bys. At my guess, Ramaseshan will be on the screen to you without much delay. Oh." Dinkuhl fished in a pocket. "A copy of your report. You'll need it."

Raven said: "Sometimes I see your point of view, Mr. Dinkuhl, and am even minded to share it. You two have now ceased to be an asset, and become instead a nuisance. Have you any good reason why I should not eliminate a nuisance?"

"The best. We're persuasive talkers. I doubt if you have an executioner you could be sure of, since we should naturally claim access to Ramaseshan. Besides, you really are very busy, Director. I should get back to your desk, if I were you."

Raven smiled. "The points are not overwhelming, but you have me. I lack the essential vindictiveness of a Chief Director; it accounts for my present awkwardness. Ramaseshan, for instance . . . Ah well. I take it you will not reconsider simply for the sake of helping me save my skin, Mr. Grayner? I thought not. What do you plan to do now, by the way?"

"Leave us to our worries," Dinkuhl said. "You have your own."

"Very true. Good-by, Mr. Grayner. I wish I could say I believed you to be in good hands. Good-by, Mr. Dinkuhl."

Walking jauntily but without haste, Raven went out.

There was no hurry this time. They went along to Oak Ridge for drinks and a meal.

"An enviable position, Charlie," Dinkuhl said. "You can even use that wrist transmitter to call up the Atomics bravos if anyone else shows awkward. For a few days you can describe yourself as in Atomics but not of it. No longer than that, I think. The Chief Director is versatile if not vindictive. He may still make a deal with Ramaseshan. Or even, for that matter, eliminate him. I told you the stakes were high."

Charles contemplated his gin and vermouth.

"Hiram," he said, "the last few weeks I have spent chasing my tail. I don't entirely blame you for this, though I do have the impression that you've provided a twist once or twice when I showed signs of slowing down, but I would have you know I'm tiring rapidly."

"Telecom came and took you. You put yourself into Atomics. I only got you out of those two havens."

"Right. For what purpose?"

"Purpose?" Dinkuhl grinned. "I'm not Raven. What do you want yourself?"

"To find Sara. If she's alive."

"O.K. Any clues?"

"None. As you know."

"As I know. Well, we've tried the overworld. I never thought we'd get anything there. Now we try the underworld."

"The underworld?"

Dinkuhl's face changed, hardened. His voice dropped an octave. "Brother," he demanded, "are you damned?" He resumed his normal expression. "After a lifetime preaching culture, I guess I can preach damnation."

"What do you expect to get from the Cometeers?"

"I don't know. Nothing. Anything. At least, it's where Contact Sections are least likely to look for us. With a couple of natural beards, we'll be impenetrable. Put not your trust in plastics when nature can lend a hand. I'll do the preaching, Charlie. You can go around with the hat."

Charles said doubtfully: "You think you can get by?"

"I've made a study of it. I'll have the rest of the preachers tearing their beards out by the roots."

"It seems crazy."

"When sanity calcifies, madness is the only solution. Any better ideas?"

Charles shook his head.

VII

THEY MOVED IN LEAPS of a hundred or a hundred and fifty miles, and at random. There was no control of the movements of the Preachers—it was their duty to travel as the spirit moved them, and they were welcome everywhere. Charles and Dinkuhl moved in a vast circular swath: east to Ohio, south to Kentucky and North Carolina, north again along the Atlantic seaboard.

Apart from one evening on Mining property, Dinkuhl had preached previously in sheds, outside the towns, belonging to Agriculture. Tonight, their gyro touched down on a waterfront section, a stretch that was apparently unused now though still nominally under the control of Telecom. It was a very decayed sector altogether, crammed with broken-down warehouses that seemed ready to slip off the waterfront into the unhealthy-looking water. The gyros already parked showed a good attendance.

They met a Preacher Robinson inside, and made their salutations. Preacher Robinson was a gaunt man and there was something odd about his speech.

"I've heard you're a fine teller of the Wrath, Preacher," he said. "Would you like to lead off?"

Dinkuhl replied: "Better if you lead off, Preacher. You've been preaching longer than I have."

Preacher Robinson inclined his head. "As you like."

He preached well, with a cold bitter fervor. But Dinkuhl, following him, was in tremendous form. The audience that had listened in silence, betraying only by

128

an occasional shuffling of feet that some charge of iniquity had sunk deeply home, was roused to a pitch of sobbing and shouting by Dinkuhl's playing on their emotions. Dinkuhl passed them back to Robinson for the liturgy that took place in the open, but, under his influence still, it was the crowd rather than the Preacher that dominated the responses.

When it was over, Charles and Dinkuhl stood beside Preacher Robinson and made their informal good-bys to the faithful. They had decided that in the presence of Robinson they would not put their usual questions about Sara and Humayun. Charles stood in silence while the two Preachers listened to the small talk and small problems of the departing congregation. The comet was plainly visible at the top of the black chasm between two warehouses. A few yards away there was the slow lap of water against rotting piles.

There was still a handful of the congregation left when Preacher Robinson started to talk. He said to Dinkuhl:

"How long have you been telling the Wrath, Preacher?"

"Not long, Preacher. The call only came to me a few weeks ago."

"You tell it well."

"An instrument of the Lord, Preacher."

Dinkuhl's voice, Charles noted, had relapsed into the drawl that signified alertness. The remaining handful of the damned had moved in closer; they were surrounded by them. There could be very little doubt that they were followers of Preacher Robinson. It was not two to one; it was two to half a dozen.

"Tell me, Preacher," Robinson said, "these other two you have been asking questions about—a woman called Koupal, a man called Humayun—are they instruments of the Lord, too?"

It might still be no more than a routine check-up; the fact that they knew of the questions they had been asking did not necessarily signify anything more than that the

129

Cometeers were a tighter-knit organization than had seemed likely on the surface.

Dinkuhl said: "Every man and every woman is an instrument of The Lord."

Preacher Robinson laughed, and his laughter was the dropping of a cloak. It was the laughter of cynicism. They had reached an inner circle; that was clear enough. And it was an inner circle dedicated to something other than the fanaticism of the Cometeers. But to what? The general inference was clear enough. Some managerial. But which? Which managerial was capable of controlling an organization like this—an organization of which Ledbetter and even Raven were unmistakably afraid?

"You put that well, Manager Dinkuhl," said Preacher Robinson. "We're still curious, all the same. What do you want Koupal and Humayun for?"

"Would you believe it," Dinkuhl drawled, "if I told you it was for no other reason than the pangs of aching love?"

"For both of them?"

"Well, one each. Charlie for Koupal and me for Humayun. It's just that I'm built that way."

Robinson laughed again. "You know," he said, "I think we'd take you in for that sense of humor, if for no other reason."

"Take us in—where?" asked Dinkuhl. "And are we expected to come willingly?"

"You'll find out where. Willingly if you like. Otherwise not. We've come prepared."

Dinkuhl groaned. "Not astarate again."

"No," Robinson said, "not astarate." He drew something out from beneath his Preacher's cloak. "We're the more primitive type."

His followers were making similar dispositions. Charles recognized what it was they carried from having seen something of the sort on a Red League historical soap opera. They were old-fashioned blackjacks.

Dinkuhl said: "Mind if I have a word with Charlie—on our own?"

130

"A word. Don't make it longer than half a minute."

Dinkuhl drew Charles to one side. "Can you swim?" Charles nodded. "The blunt instruments are all they've got; they would have produced something else if they had it. Probably don't carry anything metal in case someone puts the detectors on them. Anyway, it's worth trying a rush. There's only a couple between us and the water. Right over them and in. Swim left. There's a main artery within a hundred yards, and they can't get at us before then because of the warehouses. They won't try anything under lights."

Charles said: "O.K. When do we go?"

"We'll walk back to them and I'll take out a cigarette pack and a lighter. When I toss the lighter in the Preacher's face, we move."

The watchers appeared to relax as Charles and Dinkuhl walked back together to where Robinson stood. Dinkuhl drew his pack of cigarettes out, slowly. He felt in his pockets for the lighter.

Robinson said: "Are you prepared to be reasonable? We play ball if you do."

Dinkuhl brought out his lighter, and pressed the flame button. The small blue glow shot up to its full height of three inches.

"A lot depends," Dinkuhl observed, "on the brand of ball you play. For instance—"

He roared: "Now!" as he flicked the lighter in Robinson's face, and Charles leapt for the man immediately between himself and the waterfront. The man went down, but he brought Charles down with him. Charles rolled clear, but by the time he had got to his feet another of them had him by the arm and yet another was between him and the water. Dinkuhl had got clear. He stood by the water's edge, and looked back. They were making no attempt to go after him. Me again, Charles thought.

He called: "Beat it, Hiram!"

As he tore his arm free and dived for the man in his path, Charles saw Dinkuhl bull-rushing back to his assistance. He did not see anything else. Something hit him on the back of the head.

He came back to consciousness once to the sound of a high-pitched buzzing roar, recognizable as the noise of a stratoliner's engines. He sat up, and had time to see that he was in the hold of a cargo-plane, and tied up. Dinkuhl, also tied up, lay a little way off.

A voice said: "No trouble. We don't want trouble."

Another blackjack blow smashed him back into oblivion.

VIII

THE NEXT TIME CHARLES came to, he was free of his bonds. He sat up carefully, and then stood up. His head ached, but no more than it had done after astarate; probably the bludgeoning effect of a blackjack was no worse than that of a drug.

He was in a small neat cell of a room, but there was no question of this being a cabin in a real or fake spaceship. There was an armorplex window in one wall, and outside light came through it. His first attention was to Dinkuhl, though. Dinkuhl was lying on the floor; he had a nasty black and blue bruise on his left temple. Charles tried to rouse him, but without success. There was no water in the room, and slapping his cheeks brought no result. At least, he was alive.

Leaving him for the moment, Charles went to the window and looked out. The building they were in was on a height, and looked across a city that pricked his memory without quite yielding to it. A mixture of styles, but predominantly very old, and with more than a hint of the oriental. A museum city. That narrowed the possibilities quite a bit—there were few cities that had escaped both the War's destructions and the subsequent pattern of standardization in civic reconstruction that had marked the beginning of managerialism. He tried to think which this could be, but without being able to persuade himself of one likelihood over another. The sky was busy with gyros; that didn't help either.

It wasn't until the door of the room opened, and he saw the man who stood in the threshold that he guessed where he was. A number of things fell into place then, not least the trace of unfamiliar accent in Preacher Robinson's speech. He had never seen this man in the flesh, but he had seen a deep-view of him, and in the same dress.

It was Dai Humayun, and the dress was the Siraqi military uniform.

"You're awake," Humayun said. "But not Dinkuhl?"

"He's been roughed up badly." Charles felt his own head. "Your men seem to get some pleasure in the use of blunt instruments."

Humayun smiled. He had a slow smile that warmed his normally severe features. "The need for secrecy precluded the use of more advanced methods of repression. I won't say that some of them may not have been a little heavy-handed. Enthusiasm is a good fault in the military. But they know where to hit without doing permanent damage. And that was in their instructions— to avoid any permanent damage."

"Very thoughtful. Do you think something could be done about making Dinkuhl comfortable, now you've got us here?"

Humayun nodded. He pressed a wall button. "You have not been here long. They dropped you here, and then informed me. I came almost at once. You must have been coming around when they left you."

"Anyway, we're here." Charles gestured toward the window. "In—"

"The capital of the world." Humayun smiled again. "El Majalem. The Averroes Institute. Seventh floor. Room ninety-three. I take it you recognize me? You will have seen my records. How are things in California?"

133

"Yes, I recognized you. California—it's a few weeks since I was there."

Two orderlies, also in uniform, brought a stretcher in. Humayun said: "He should have been taken to sickbay. See that he's looked after."

As they left the room, Charles said urgently: "Sara—she's all right?" Humayun nodded. "And her father?"

The remark amused Humayun. "Yes. Professor Koupal is in good health and spirits. Very good spirits. He wants to see you."

"And Sara?"

"That's a matter for Professor Koupal. We'll go along now, if you're ready."

Charles held his hands up. The rope had cut deeply, and it had been oily. "A wash would be useful."

"Yes, of course. Our sanitary arrangements are not quite managerial, but I have a lavatory attached to my office here. Come on down."

Humayun's office was two floors below; they went down and Humayun showed him to the lavatory.

"You'll find me back in the office when you're ready," he told him. "Soap, towels—got everything?"

Charlies tidied himself up as well as he could, and went out to rejoin Humayun. He got up from his desk, and then sat down again.

"Something you may be interested in, before we go along to Government House. Have a cigarette? Take a chair."

The cigarette was very welcome, and Charles was not reluctant to sit down. He glanced around the office. Nothing unusual, except that it was rather untidy. There was a TV screen inset in the wall.

Humayun spoke into some kind of tube: that was new.

He said: "Get me Gathenya." He glanced up at Charles. "We use wire more than you do for communications. A result of being closely knit and centralized. There's a saving on power, and we have had to learn ways of economy."

134

The screen lit up to show a man sitting at a desk. He apparently recognized Humayun, and saluted him.

Humayun spoke to him in French, and he nodded. *"Oui, General."* The screen blanked, and opened up again to show a factory interior. It was a mass-production layout, but not automated: there seemed to be far too many workers. Humayun said something else in French, and the cameras switched to a close view of the end of the line. The products were being picked off the line and carefully stacked for transfer somewhere else. They were small, metal, egg-shaped.

"Recognize them?"

Charles shook his head. "Should I?"

Humayun gave another instruction in French. This time the scene cut to a courtyard, enclosed but open to the sky. It was filled with a swarm of monstrous bees. Men flying.

These, too, wore Siraqi military uniform. Each was encased in a skeletal framework of metal. The framework had a footrest, a seat, and a waistband with certain controls. From the waistband the metal rose in a hoop above the flyer's head. At the top of the hoop were the vanes; horizontal for take-off and inclinable in various directions for routine flying and maneuver. As the scene became more clearly visualized in Charles' mind, he understood that quite a complicated aerial parade was taking place. One flyer, hovering motionless at one end of the courtyard, was an instructor; the rest were obeying his commands.

"A very neat design," he commented at last. "Powered by . . . ?"

"As you will have guessed, by the diamond-solar battery. Those were the batteries you have just seen coming off the assembly line."

"Congratulations. But I don't know how you did it, in the time. I saw at least six months' work in the development stage, quite apart from the time required for production—tooling up, and so on."

Humayun smiled. "Of course. That's why I can't accept

135

the congratulations. We have had people working here on it right from the beginning. My job at San Diego was a stalling one for the last year. Not as easy as you might think."

Charles looked at him sceptically. "Two questions. How could you have people working on this here in Siraq, when you and the Koupals were refugees? And if you did have them, why give any information at all to United Chemicals? You gave enough to interest more than one managerial."

"So I understand. The answer to the first question is that this is a capitalist country, not a managerial one. Disorganized, ramshackle, inefficient. So inefficient that it was not at all difficult to carry out research work unknown to the government of the time. Professor Koupal was Director of this Institute before our misfortune. The President was badly misinformed; the man he appointed in succession was one of our group. It was quite easy to camouflage the work.

"As for your second question, the idea was in a very embryonic stage indeed when we left Siraq. I needed a laboratory and funds very urgently. I had to wave some kind of carrot under the noses of those donkeys at Graz. And I had to continue to give them enough to persuade them to maintain the project—though I understand a good deal of what I did send was being intercepted by Ledbetter for another managerial?"

Charles nodded. Humayun went on: "And I was fairly confident that there wasn't one of them with the training and brains to make anything of the information, anyway. From what Sara told me about you, I discovered that I had made a mistake there. Our men tried to locate you, but various other groups got on to you first. I should be interested to learn why they didn't manage to keep you. Anyway, you dropped very neatly into our hands."

"Into your hands?"

"The Cometeers."

"The Cometeers are a Siraqi organization?"

"Let's say, we provided the first spark for the powder

136

trail. Its success has rather overwhelmed us. Our psychological advisers plotted it out, but I think even they have been surprised by the results. The present membership figures are astonishing, and there's a steep upward curve for the rate of increase."

"The instruments used by Siraq are not such that they commend Siraq to me," Charles said.

Humayun shrugged. "A pity. Unfortunately, the Cometeers are necessary to our plans. We aren't fond of them ourselves, but at the same time they could never have succeeded unless the society in which they flourished was corrupt. And there's another point. We expect them to be the means of saving thousands, perhaps hundreds of thousands of lives. The majority of them not Siraqi."

"In what way?"

"You will be told, I fancy. We should be getting along. There's one other thing you might be interested in first."

Humayun spoke into the tube again, and again the TV picture changed. A larger courtyard. More of the flyers. They watched them drop down toward a row of black canisters laid out at about three-yard intervals on the ground. The frameworks supporting these flyers carried on each side a small barrel-like affair, terminating in a nozzle. Suddenly, and presumably at a word of command because the effects were nearly simultaneous, there was a lambent flickering around each of the nozzles, and on the ground the canisters—or all but two of them—burst into flame.

"The heat ray," said Humayun. "Beloved by managerial TV serial writers. The other diamond application. Unfortunately limited to use in conditions of sunlight, but, granted those conditions, most effective. Variable focus, but only between certain limits, of course, and the range is not very great. The heat, at point of impact, is. I won't give you a figure, because I don't think you would believe me. A surprise, you think?"

"Only in its actual appearance," Charles said grimly. "A few people have grasped the idea."

137

"Then they will be surprised, to see their idea marching on the wings of the wind."

Humayun switched off the screen, and got up to go. Charles said: "One thing. How much of all this did Sara know—when she was with you at San Miguel?"

"Our conventions are perhaps peculiar. There are some things we don't regard as suitable for women—they include counter-revolution and military strategy. Sara didn't know anything."

Humayun said: "May I present you? Charles Grayner —Professor Koupal, President of Siraq."

The gyro had brought them to the grounds of a modest little house on the outskirts of El Majalem, and the room in which they now were was as unassuming. Professor Koupal got up to greet them from a scratched and shabby desk; there was no large TV screen in the room, but a portable callscreen beside the desk. Professor Koupal smiled, and Charles remembered and recognized the humorous slyness he had seen on the morning of Sara's disappearance.

Professor Koupal said: "Our apologies, Charles. I hear you've been somewhat roughly handled, too. That wasn't intended. We've been inculcating aggressiveness into our soldiers, and it's difficult to prevent them from overdoing it at times."

"President?" Charles asked. "Since when? I haven't been seeing the newsreels very lately."

"Would your newsreels regard it as worth the recording? I suppose they might. But this has been a very secret palace revolution. We thought it best not to let the news leak out just yet. The *coup d'état* coincided with Dai's return here. It was well planned and went without a hitch. I was called back when it was all over."

"Sara—"

"I felt it was necessary to bring Sara with me. There were a number of good reasons for that, not the least being her value as a hostage if left behind. She expressed unwillingness when I told her." Professor Koupal looked

138

at Charles keenly. "She wanted to tell you, but of course that was impossible. I was afraid she might have left some clue, though I took all precautions."

Charles remembered the incident of the finger-watch; with the false-Sara's explanation out of the way, it assumed its earlier importance. He smiled slightly.

"I gather she did," Professor Koupal said. "Well, never mind that now. The point of all the preparations was to throw United Chemicals, and any other managerial that happened to be interested, off the scent. We seem to have been helped by the local rivalry; even when the genuineness of the deaths was suspected, they were too eager to lay the blame at each other's doors."

Charles nodded. Only now was he beginning to grasp the scope of the plan underlying the work of Humayun, the disappearances, his own abduction. Keeping his voice even, he said:

"The idea, I suppose, is of some sort of aggression by Siraq against the rest of the world—a foray for fresh territory." Professor Koupal was smiling at him benignly. "How long has that been in preparation?"

"A very long time. On an old Japanese analogy, Dai and I were members of the war party. There was a peace party; our temporary eviction was the result of a temporary defeat in an earlier skirmish. The position has now been rectified."

"You want war. Why?"

Professor Koupal raised his hands. "Wanting doesn't enter into it. The world outside is breaking up. There will be chaos there, anyway, within a couple of decades, and, as the only state with any vitality at all, we should have to go out then and reclaim the chaos. It would be a long job and a painful one—unnecessarily so. It is simpler, and a lot more efficient, to precipitate matters. Has Dai mentioned the Cometeers to you? We've found confirmation for our views there, and it is of great help in the softening-up."

Charles said: "Let me see if I can understand what you

139

are talking about. You mean—Siraq taking the whole planet over?"

"Exactly."

"With a handful of aerial soldiers and a heat ray that only works at close quarters, and when the sun happens to be shining?"

"I should put it somewhat higher than that," Professor Koupal said judiciously. "Let me explain something of the art of warfare to you, Charles. That art, throughout the centuries, has seen a continual alternation in the status of the individual warrior, through the alternation in the kind of weapons at man's disposal. To render the situation down, you may say that artillery dwarfs the individual soldier, while small-arms magnifies him. Of course, you can pick your own variations of the theme, from the conflict between the giant sling and the javelin in Roman times, to the conflict between the big guns and the musket in the eighteenth century.

"During the twentieth century, the balance swung—irretrievably as it seemed—away from the soldier. Massed artillery barrages, pattern bombing, and finally the atomic and hydrogen bombs seemed to tilt the scales finally toward the mass-weapon. And weapons, of course, affect society. The musket was typical of capitalism, just as the H-bomb is typical of managerialism, even though it was the last stage of world capitalism that produced it."

"The managerial world," Charles observed, "still has a stock of H-bombs."

"Which are quite useless. The mass-weapon has grown too big to use. Yes, I know it was used in the last war, but the results bear me out, don't they? Do you think your friends will use H-bombs? On what targets? We shall have Africa within a week, Europe within ten days. Do you know what the situation resembles? It resembles a small iron-walled room, full of big men holding Klaberg pistols. And a child comes in with a water-pistol and drenches them. They can't hit back because they haven't got any water-pistols, and wouldn't know how to use them if they had. And if they fire their pistols, the charges will ricochet off the walls; they are as likely as not to kill themselves, and they know it."

"As far as I can see, a longbow would out-shoot your new weapon, Professor Koupal."

Professor Koupal smiled. "And which managerial has a stock of longbows? I take your point, though. The heat ray is not the weapon that restores the initiative to the soldier. The flying apparatus is. We've had the essential design for some time, but it's heavy on power—as you might expect. The sun, fortunately, is an inexhaustible power-house. That makes the weapon worth having. Wings on every soldier. A flying army. Even without the added advantages of surprise and an enemy that has, in the main, lost interest in everything but its hypothetical damnation, this new factor would be sufficient to do the trick. In all probability. We have taken the elementary precaution of mapping out the key points. There isn't one that can't be taken by half a dozen of our flying soldiers. And we have more than that to spare."

They could do it, too. Charles could visualize the situation very clearly. The Cometeers running hog-wild . . . he had already learned that a Cometeer did not pause to consider managerial loyalty when a call came in the name of The Lord . . . and then the trained, disciplined and efficient Siraqi troops dropping through the air . . . It was a cast-iron scheme. Understanding this, it occurred to him to wonder why it had all been explained to him. His skill wasn't wanted now. The only advantage he represented to Siraq was the negative one—assurance that he would not be doing anything for the managerials.

He said: "One thing interests me." Professor Koupal raised his head slightly. "Why you have told me all this."

"A reasonable question. Because I am going to ask you to give me your parole." Charles looked baffled. "An old expression—your promise of honor that you will not try to escape or communicate with anyone outside Siraq. That given, you will have a good deal of liberty. And if you are to give it, I think you must be told enough of your situation to make its implications clear to you. This

141

is the world's new capital. We want you to understand that."

"How long before you attack?"

"Not long."

That startled him. "Now—in winter? It will take the edge off your weapon, won't it?"

"Unfortunately. Though not as much as you might think. The cloud is generally low at this time of year, and it will not be difficult to rise above cloud height for recharging."

Charles, with a twinge midway between guilt and regret, thought of airsphering with the false-Sara, and the world of blue and gold and stillness.

"But in any case," Professor Koupal went on, "timing is now a matter of some urgency. It isn't that we have any fears of the managerials duplicating the battery or the weapon within six months—for that matter, within six decades—but they might get round to suspecting the true state of affairs, given six months' grace. We can't bank on their mutual mistrust holding out. And surprise is going to be very important. So we shall go ahead in the very near future."

"In which case," Charles said, "surely it would be simpler to keep me under lock and key?"

Professor Koupal smiled benevolently. "There are personal considerations."

Sara. It was a warming thought. As though he had been tunneling toward her for months, through miles of rock and had become aware of a tapping, answering him and directly ahead. At the same time—

He said: "I'd like to have the opportunity of talking things over with Dinkuhl."

Professor Koupal nodded. "Naturally. Dai will take you back."

Dinkuhl was sitting up in bed, in a small but not unattractive room. There was a table beside his bed, with a large bowl full of fruit on it. Dinkuhl grinned wryly.

"Come to devour the grapes?"

Humayun said: "I'll leave you here, Charles. I'm afraid we have to post a guard outside, for the time being. He will take you to me whenever you want that."

"Adios," Dinkuhl said. "Back to the detector screen? Why not just crawl under the bed?"

Humayun looked puzzled for a moment. "Oh, I get it. No, you're private in here. Our privacy regulations forbid the installation of detector equipment."

He smiled and went out. Dinkuhl looked after him.

"You know," he said, "I believe he's telling the truth."

"Probably. How are you feeling?"

Dinkuhl rubbed his head gingerly. "Regretful. Death was more welcome. But it will pass. The number who takes my pulse will help it to pass, I feel."

Charles said: "It will need to. You will need all your faculties to think up a scheme for getting us out of this."

Dinkuhl's look was quizzical. "Maybe you'd better let me have anything you know."

He listened in silence while Charles told him what he had been told by Humayun and Professor Koupal. He said at last:

"I can think of one thing that's likely to prevent them from doing it."

Charles said eagerly: "Yes?"

"The sun blowing up." Dinkuhl looked at him. "Relax, Charlie boy. You want my advice? Give your parole. And then enjoy yourself."

The flippancy was the same, but it didn't seem to be the same Dinkuhl. In the past the flippancy had been only the cover for a mind driving hard on its course. He examined Dinkuhl's features more closely; he thought he could detect something he had never seen there before: indifference that somehow was more harsh than despair.

Dinkuhl took an orange and began to peel it. "Help yourself, Charlie."

Charles said: "I don't know about getting out of Siraq. The odds are against us. In fact, they're so much against us that a more limited objective might be a good deal easier than it seems on the surface."

143

Dinkuhl dropped a curl of peel on the floor. "A limited objective?"

"I don't believe there is a detector on this room. It's part of the business of one guard outside the door, of being taken around by Humayun, in person and alone. They are so confident that we couldn't get out of the country that they take hardly any precautions on the spot. Listen, Hiram. This building is served for TV by a single transmitter-receiver room. I know where it is because Humayun took me past it and the door was open. There is only one duty operator—I suppose they can manage with one because so much is covered by landlines."

Dinkuhl sectioned his orange. "I am ahead of you by a neck. We are in the TV room. We have laid out the solitary operator. Pick it up from there."

"To my mind there's only one man who might be able to do anything worth while with the information we could give him."

"Raven?"

"Yes. Do you agree?"

Dinkuhl nodded: "I agree."

Charles said: "Right. I suggest we call the guard in, and I'll stand behind the door and hit him as he comes in. It may be elementary, but I think it will work."

Dinkuhl shook his head. "Charlie boy, it's you should be in bed. Wait till I recover a little more, and you can have it. I'll go get the nurse for you. Don't thank me. It will be a pleasure."

"What's wrong with the idea?"

"Look," Dinkuhl said. "You wanted the girl. You're within ten minutes of her. You only have to go and tell Humayun you are retiring from the cloak and dagger business. You never were cut out for it, anyway."

"You won't come in on this?"

"The nail goes to the woodwork in. I won't."

"You'll be content to see the Siraqis running the world?"

144

"That nurse can run me any day. The hell with the world."

"I'm serious."

"That's your bad luck. I lost my girlish laughter too long ago to be serious at my time of life. Lookit, Charlie, you've got what you wanted."

Charles paused. He said slowly: "What about you, Hiram? What was it you wanted?"

There was another silence. Dinkuhl said: "O.K. What did I want? Your girl for you? I wish I could rate myself as high for altruism. I told you once, Charlie—you were the H-bomb. You were what was going to blow the top off. You were the Destruction, and I served the Destruction. You aren't now, are you? Go in peace, brother, if go you must."

"You've found a bigger bomb?"

"Just that. Now I wait. I don't know what I wait for, but I wait. I don't kid myself the Siraqis have got much more than the managerials, except in the military line, but it looks like being an interesting year. Go and get the word through to Raven, if your loyalties are still stronger than your common sense. I don't say it won't affect the issue. But it will still be an interesting year, whatever you do."

Charles looked toward the door.

"I'm a neutral," Dinkuhl said. "I won't call for nurse. That's a big sacrifice I'm making, the way I feel right now."

Charles called out to the guard. His own voice seemed unnatural to him. He posted himself behind the door, grasping, by its projecting handle, the heavy wooden fruit bowl; he had emptied the fruits on to Dinkuhl's bed. Dinkuhl was watching with every sign of interest.

The door opened and the guard came in. He wasn't very tall; it was an easy matter to crash the bowl down on the back of his head. He pitched forward in a falling arc and hit the floor with a cracking thud. Dinkuhl leaned down to look at him.

"Pretty. I see now what they mean about the spectator

seeing the wood for the trees. You have at least quarter of an hour, Charlie boy. I should take the bowl with you."

The corridor was deserted and it was no more than ten yards to the service lift. He called it down, and got in with relief—leaving the scene of the crime. The TV room was ground floor. He made his movements in closing the lift gate studied and deliberate. There were two or three people in this corridor, between him and his quarry. He walked along, swinging the fruit bowl casually. A girl looked at him curiously as he passed her, but no more.

The door of the TV room was closed now. That was bad luck. Fortunately whistle locks did not seem to be in use in Siraq. The door had a handle; he was going to turn it when he found it gave under the pressure of his hand. He pushed it open, gently.

The operator was sitting at the main control panel with his back to the door. He had not yet become aware of the open door, but he might at any moment. Charles ran toward him, raising the fruit bowl above his head as he did so. The operator turned around, in time to take the blow on his forehead, instead of on the base of his skull. It was as effective. His breath exhaled in a dull groan and he slumped forward onto his desk.

Charles went back and closed the door. It had a lock on this side—an old-fashioned key lock—and he secured it. Then he went back and examined the operator; he was out, all right. On the panel in front of the desk a spotlight lit up a figure 21. Someone wanting attention. How long could he count on before someone came to see why there was no response? Perhaps as long as it would take the guard to come around in Dinkuhl's room. The point was, with a meagre knowledge of TV communications, to get on to the outside circuits and get Raven in that time.

It would have been easy with Dinkuhl, of course.

It took him five minutes to master the controls to the extent of getting through to Athens, the nearest managerial booster station. He had rolled the operator onto the floor, out of sight of the screen.

The sight of the neat chrome-and-plastic Telecom desk stirred strange feelings; after recent events and the time spent earlier with the Cometeers, he had almost forgotten what it would look like. The operator was a girl; above the neat uniform her face had the typical dreamy remoteness of a mesc-taker. She registered no surprise at his bearded and disheveled appearance; after all she would take him for a Siraqi, and would hardly be surprised at anything.

He said: "El Majalem for Atomics HQ, Philadelphia."

Even that did not surprise her, although it was a safe bet that that particular link was not made once in a decade. She said sleepily:

"El Majalem for Philadelphia. Stand by, El Majalem."

He said: "It's urgent."

She smiled and barely nodded. "Yuh."

He thought, while he watched her making the call to the space station that would provide the junction between the world's continents, of what Raven would do when he gave him the news. He would put it on record, of course, to carry weight at the Council meeting he would have to call. The managerials, under such a threat, would be forced into unity. They would have to unite, if they were to defend themselves.

And then? The Siraqis would go through with it—they had gone too far to draw back now. A bitter war, a long war. They would be unlikely to save Africa; Europe might go, too. But the Americas were defensible, especially if Raven took the obvious precaution of rounding up the leaders of the Cometeers.

For Raven, it would be a good war: the natural, the automatic leader. His thoughts were wrily humorous. Let Raven have it. All he wanted himself was peace of mind: the feeling that, dragged from obscurity into temporary greatness, he had kept his faith with the society that had bred him—whether shot through with evil, whether condemned to die despite everything, he

147

had kept faith. For that he was willing to let the rest go—his personal liberty, his life if they required it . . . and Sara.

The girl was talking again, though not to him.

"Station Q Five? Athens has a call for Philadelphia."

Was there a discrepancy between his action now, and his refusal to stay with Raven and work for Atomics in the past? Perhaps, perhaps not. Raven had seen catastrophe coming, but Raven's word had been suspect. And it had been a different catastrophe even so. Civil war is something you never believe in until it breaks out. So is the collapse of a state from within. It was the outside shock that stimulated half-forgotten patriotism.

It was hard to think of losing Sara when he had come so very close to finding her again. So hard that he mistrusted his ability to keep his purpose steeled if he did think of that. The picture was plaguing him now; he thrust it back, finding crazy jingles of thought to keep it at bay. "Raven the Raven, Raven's ravin'—"

"Raven's ravin—"

It became a real thought, with the clear sharpness of ice. What would Raven do? Call the Council—round up the leaders of the Cometeers? He saw suddenly that he would do nothing so half-hearted as that; he had been underestimating Raven. Professor Koupal had been contemptuous of the H-bomb because by the time the managerials had awakened to the fact of invasion, the airborne Siraqi armies would be all over Africa and Europe. In those conditions it would be impossible to use the H-bomb. But Charles was creating different conditions—the Siraqis still locked within their relatively small territory were a target impossible to miss. Raven would not miss it.

Well, he thought—my life, if they require it. He had lost Sara, anyway.

The girl said: "Philadelphia coming in, El Majalem. They will be transferred as soon as focused."

It hit him so hard that for a moment there seemed to be blackness before his eyes.

. . . Sara was in the target.

The girl said: "In focus. Will you accept, El Majalem?"

He stared at the screen, wondering what it was he had been going to do. He heard her voice again, mesctolerant and weary:

"Philadelphia is in focus, El Majalem. Are you ready to accept the call?"

To the right of the desk there was the building's code of numbers. Humayan was 71.

"Philadelphia . . ." the voice began again.

He didn't look up. He said: "Cancel it."

She said: "O.K. Canceled."

The picture faded. He connected to 71. He said, when Humayun answered:

"This is Grayner. I'm in the TV room. You can come and collect me."

Looking at her, he wondered how he could ever have been taken in by the false-Sara. The thing about her was not the lines of her face, her body, but the sparkle, the altogether inimitable glint of personality. And, although she was smiling, she was watching him warily; how could he have forgotten that wariness which was more a part of Sara than the tiny bulges just above her eyebrows? He remembered the flesh, peeled off by Dinkuhl's knife . . . it should not have needed that.

He said humbly: "I've been getting into trouble, Sara, since I lost you."

She laughed. "If being just on the point of calling down H-bombs on us is to be labeled as getting into trouble . . . anyway, you didn't."

"There was more to it than that . . . I meant, back in North America. I didn't think of H-bombs. That call I tried to make,"—he looked directly at her—"I was prepared to not see you again, Sara. I didn't want it to happen—the take-over—with any consent of mine. You understand?"

"Within limits." She patted the plastifoam couch. "Come and sit down." She was wearing the very full

149

skirt which was the common dress of Siraqi women, and she drew it away to let him sit by her. "The other trouble. Details?"

He told her about the false-Sara; it was a relief to make confession. Sara said thoughtfully:

"You went airsphering with her?"

He nodded. "Yes." He wondered if he looked as uneasy as he felt; he supposed so.

"It's a very romantic occupation. A cousin of mine did a thesis on the aphrodisiacal effects of airsphering. He had to go outside Siraq for the practical work, of course . . . our young ladies don't go airsphering except with their fiancés. He went to Greece."

Charles looked at her unhappily. "Yes?"

"The correlation was positive." Sara paused. "Tell me. What was I like?"

"It was a very good disguise. Just like you, physically—of course, they had had access to your records. But I shouldn't have been deceived by it. It wasn't you, Sara."

"Not even in the airsphere, high above the clouds?"

He grinned shamefacedly. "Least of all, then. I was surprised."

"But pleased, I guess." She got up from the couch and stood facing him; the trace of a smile made her face expressionless. She leaned forward slightly and slapped him, stingingly hard, on either cheek. He put his hand up and rubbed first one side and then the other. She stood looking at him.

"What was that for?"

The smile deepened, but he still could not read the inward expression. She said:

"The first was on behalf of the other Sara. She should have done it, so I'm doing it for her. The second was on my own account—for your still having thought it was me, afterward."

He nodded, in gloom. "I'm sorry."

"Sorry! What about doing something to show you really are sorry?"

He looked up. "I'll do anything, Sara."

150

He thought her composure was going to desert her for a moment; there was the beginning of embarrassment, but she controlled it. She said brusquely:

"This afternoon then . . . you can take me airsphering."

He grasped her hand, and she let him pull her down beside him on the couch again. She averted her face from his kisses, but she was smiling happily now. He hesitated in the attempt as a thought struck him.

"But you said . . . no airsphering except with—"

"—Fiancés. Idiot! Don't you realize you are being proposed to?"

He drew her to him, and now she took his kisses, and kissed him back. When, after some minutes, he released her, he offered her his cheek.

She looked at him thoughtfully. "Well?"

"Since you are going to marry me, I'd prefer to get all my punishment over in advance. I went airsphering more than once."

Sara raised her eyebrows. "How many times?"

"About half a dozen."

She looked at his offered face, and at her hand.

"No. Not just yet. A good wife always keeps something in reserve."

The Director's garden on the roof of the Averroes Institute was almost exclusively made up of evergreens and roses; the roses were made to bloom all the year round so the seasons did not touch it. From the garden, on this morning, it was a small party that looked out, away from the center of El Majalem, toward the military camp on the outskirts. The party was made up of Professor Koupal and Humayun, Sara and Charles, and Dinkuhl. The sky was a sparkling blue, and the great sun itself dimmed, by comparison, the sunlets that were strung above their heads.

Professor Koupal said: "Dai has been telling me about your idea, Charles. We'd considered the idea of utilizing the space stations as solar power collectors, of course, but the distribution is impossible. They can collect all right, but the only power they use is for TV boosting. We can't run cables up to them.

"This idea of yours—of maintaining a collector on airspheres; it might work. We could run cables there, for reasonably low cloud levels at any rate. There's one thing—wouldn't they drift?"

"They couldn't if they were cabled, could they? At least, not far. The airspheres take care of the buoyancy, and the cables take care of the drift. You could have an operator up there, as well."

Professor Koupal nodded his head. "Cheap power all the year round. Make a big difference in the cloudy territories—the British Isles, and so on. What do you think, Dai?"

"Very nice. I can foresee some lively problems. I suggest this presents a good first job for the Bhaldun lab."

Sara protested: "Let's get over the honeymoon first. We haven't officially accepted Bhaldun yet."

Humayun said: "I speak with my full military authority." He grinned. "Any recalcitrance and I'll split you—Charles to Cairo and you to Constantinople. I can make that opposing hemispheres once the take-over is accomplished."

"Managerialist!" Sara said. "We wouldn't go."

Professor Koupal said: "It's a pity we can't do anything about utilizing power in space. Such a waste. But short of developing a power transmitter, it can't be done."

Charles said: "There's one way of utilizing it."

"And that is . . . ?"

"Atomic-powered spaceships are clumsy and hellishly expensive. Diamond-solar power would make them a different proposition altogether."

Professor Koupal nodded slowly. Humayun said:

"Get thee to Bhaldun. Delay the honeymoon."

"Delay the spaceships," Sara said. "First things come first."

Charles said: "What about you, Hiram? Decided on anything yet?"

The indifference that Charles had first noticed behind Dinkuhl's ordinary flippancy, when he tried to persuade him to join him in warning Raven, now, for the most part, had taken its place. He did not talk very much, and then laconically.

He said: "I'm not sure."

Humayun said: "I've offered him the job of running the Telecom units, as we take them over. It's still open."

Charles asked: "What about it, Hiram?"

Dinkuhl appeared to rouse himself. "Very kind of everybody. I guess I'm not an organizer, though."

Charles said: "When we first met in this business—in Detroit—you said you had thought of trying to get KF transferred to Siraq. Well, here you are. Why not?"

"A misconception," Dinkuhl said. "KF was a legacy from capitalism—Siraq was capitalist. I missed the nuances. KF stemmed from philanthropic capitalism, from capitalism in decay. Siraq is a different kind of capitalism. Military capitalism, maybe. Nearer to the roots, anyway. And the root of capitalism is giving people what they want—what they want, not what they ought to want. They never wanted KF, except the cranks, and a sane and healthy society doesn't cater for the cranks."

Charles said: "Isn't there anything you want?"

"There is one thing—"

Humayun looked at his finger-watch. "I think . . . now!"

They looked. From the camp the leather-jacketed swarm was rising, like locusts, into the sharp blue sky. At this moment, throughout the Siraqi territory, similar swarms were setting out. Like locusts they would fasten on the neighboring lands, stripping them of their nerves and moving relentlessly on. Locusts with intelligence, locusts with a purpose. The kaleidoscope of civilization was being shaken; one could only guess into what new pattern it might settle, or whether there would be a pattern.

"Mankind is on the move again," said Professor Koupal.

"They'll get by," Dinkuhl said. "Mankind is like Charlie; mankind is adaptable. You'll be happy at Bhaldun, Charlie. A wife and a line of research—two lines of research. What more could you want? I hope you're glad I didn't come in with you on the last break. There was no one I wanted to save from the H-bomb."

"You had thought of that? Why didn't you, then? You wanted destruction."

The swarm had already become a cloud on the horizon, a fading cloud. Dinkuhl gestured toward it.

"I prefer it spread well out."

Humayun said: "I interrupted you just now. You were going to say there was something you wanted. If we can provide it, it's yours."

Dinkuhl nodded. "Very kind of you. It isn't much. I'd like the use of a camel."

CODA

It was a part of the country from which even the aggressive Siraqi agriculture had fallen back in dismay—rocky barren ground useless for everything except grazing sheep. He had passed several flocks, tended by young boys who would presumably grow into the leather jackets that awaited them, the sun-powered wings. But this section was deserted. Dinkuhl was alone, with the camel and his thoughts. He had grown used by now to the uneasy rocking motion of his passage, and to the camel's grunts, the flapping pad of its feet and what he suspected was the creaking of its joints.

It was night. Stars, but no moon. The stars themselves were big and brilliant in a cloudless sky. Weather, he reflected, was still on the side of Siraq. He wondered where the locusts had reached by now—Cape Town, Gibraltar, London, Moscow, Delhi?

The comet looked very big, too, and almost overhead. Great for the Cometeers. He tried to rouse disgust, or even the more detached feeling of ironical contempt, but indifference possessed him and would not be set aside. Indifference was a good armor, but a poor companion. A close one, though, and a determined one.

Indifference had come with the death of hope, and hope had died with the news Charlie had brought him, in the little room at the Averroes Institute. He had not known it then, because he had not known that hope had been with him at all, but he had understood it later.

"Destroy!" his mind had said. "Destroy!" He had not heard its quieter whisper: "That good may come from the casting down of evil."

And suddenly he had seen Destruction in the wings, ready to move on stage, and he saw it for what it was—an ordinary player, supplanting, but essentially no different from the other players. And hope had died, unrecognized.

The Siraqis, the Managerialists, the Cometeers. . . . There was nothing to despair of losing, and so there could be nothing to hope for. Was there hope without despair? Hope for hope's sake? His mind cried irrationally: "Stay with me! Stay with me, anyway!"

Hope came with innocence, and went with knowledge. And can a man unlearn what he has learned?

"Stay with me!" his mind cried again. "Let me be a child, but stay with me. I was willing to give up everything to despair, except my knowledge. Take that, too, if I can have hope."

He rode his swaying camel under the frost-bright stars. Ahead he could see the lights of a village, a small village but lit as though for carnival. He could hear voices singing; it was puzzling, because the village was still too far away for the songs to be from there. The voices were nearer, and at last he saw the singers, coming toward him along the stony path. They were young lads, shepherds.

They were rejoicing, and he was happy in their happiness. He tried to catch the words of their song, but he had very little understanding of the dialect. As they came abreast of him, he called out to them:

"What is the name of this village?"

Several of them answered him, but he knew what name it would be before they said it. He pricked the camel with the goad, urging it to greater speed.

He said aloud, crying to the black sky, to the stars, to the plunging comet:

158

"I was ready to give up knowledge for hope. And now hope and knowledge are the same."

From the rag-bag of memory he found words—words that it surprised him to remember.

"Nunc dimittis . . ."

London: 24 · iv · 54.

for the best in fantasy

and science-fiction reading

don't fail to read these Avon books.

WE WHO SURVIVED
by Sterling Noel

An Avon Original novel by one of America's masters of suspense, WE WHO SURVIVED is a gripping, horror-streaked tale of tomorrow that begins on a cold, brooding Saturday in September, 2203 . . . the day the snow began to fall—and did not stop!

T-360 {35¢}

THE MAN WHO COULD CHEAT DEATH
by Barre Lyndon & Jimmy Sangster

The startling story of Dr. Georges Bonner, who solved the mystery of eternal life but didn't realize the terrible price he had to pay—until the day he had to kill to stay alive!

T-362 {35¢}

BEYOND THE NIGHT
by Cornell Woolrich

Six tales of horror to flutter the heart and chill the mind by Cornell Woolrich (also known as William Irish), who has long been unique in his uncanny blending of humdrum reality with sheer horror outside the bounds of reason.

T-354 {35¢}